CLASSIC PULP FICTION

HOME FOR KILLERS! .... Charles Boeckman   3
A man can run just so far before facing the devil in pursuit.

THUBWAY THAM'S BAGGAGE CHECK .... Johnston McCulley 13
Detective Craddock tags along to the pickpocket's hometown.

SPACE BURIAL .... Lew Merrill 23
His enemy challenged him five astronomical units from earth.

THE ROBBERS .... E.C. Tubb 39
A new breed of soldier from the ashes of the pioneers ...

THE COLOUR OUT OF SPACE .... H.P. Lovecraft 99
Had Death descended from the stars?

THEFT OF THE CROWN JEWELS .... John Clemons 121
A Dastardly Swindle in Stones Takes Shape!

NEW PULP FICTION

SNIFFING OUT THE RAIN SHADOW .... Robert W. Walker 57
A cadaver dog goes forth on a rescue mission ...

GIVE 'EM HELL, HELEN .... Adam McFarlane 65
The race was on, but was Helen racing to or from something?

THE OCCURRENCE OF THE KALI CURSE ... Teel James Glenn 73

GREAT CAESAR'S GHOST .... Jack Halliday 91

DEPARTMENTS

Editorial .... Rich Harvey 2
"Remembering E.C. ('Ted') Tubb" .... Philip Harbottle 53
Retro Review: *The Big Fix* by Ed Lacy .... Rich Harvey 138

Issue #35
Spring 2020

Rich Harvey, *Publisher*
Audrey Parente, *Editor*

Cover
Ozni Brown
True Detective, February 1953

"Home for Killers!"
Copyright © 1952 Charles Beckman.
© Renewed 1970 Patti Beckman.
All rights reserved.

"Sniffing Out the Rain Shadow"
© 2018 Robert W. Walker.
All rights reserved.
First published in as "Sniff Sniff"
in 'Off the Beaten Path' #3
(Prospective Press, 2018)

"Give 'Em Hell, Helen"
© 2020 Adam Beau McFarlane.
All rights reserved.

"Occurrence of the Kali Curse"
© 2020 Teel James Glenn.
All rights reserved.

"Great Caesar's Ghost"
© 2020 Jack Halliday.
All rights reserved.

"Remembering E.C. ("Ted") Tubb"
© 2020 Philip Harbottle.
All rights reserved.

"Retro Review"
© 2020 Rich Harvey.
All rights reserved.

"The Robbers"
Copyright © 1954 by E.C. Tubb.
Reprinted by permission of
Cosmos Literary Agency
for the author's estate.

Pulp Adventures TM & © 2020 Bold Venture Press All rights reserved. Published quarterly. The stories in this publication are fiction (except for "Remembering E.C. ["Ted"] Tubb"). Any similarities to actual persons, living or dead, is purely coincidental. 0601

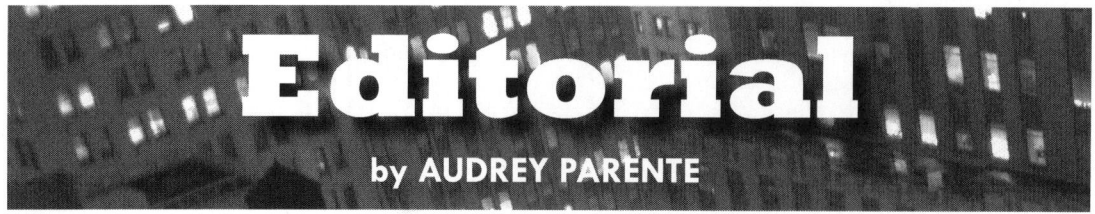

Editorial
by AUDREY PARENTE

Bold Venture Press was humbled recently by an unexpected recognition of our *Pulp Adventures #29*, which has reinforced our motive to reprint and respect "old pulp" while recognizing and publishing great "new pulp."

Pulp Adventures #29 reprinted stories from early pulp authors Charles Boeckman (*Famous Detective Stories* 1955), Theodore Roscoe (*Action Stories*, 1941), Albert Richard Wetjen (*Action Stories* 1941) and Laurence Donovan (*Speed Western Stories* 1946). The "new pulp" writers in the issue were Andrew Bourelle, Jack Bludis under his pen name Jack Burns, Adam Beau McFarlane, David Bernard, the late Johnny Strike, Gary Lovisi and Rie Sheridan Rose. The issue used original pulp art but also introduced a new pulp fiction artist Aleena Valentine-Lopez.

The recognition came from the back-cover story of *Pulp Adventures #29*, which highlighted contemporary new-pulp author Andrew Bourelle's story "The Gentleman's Exit."

The author and his story were listed in Otto Penzler's book, *The Best American Mystery Stories 2019*, under "Other Distinguished Mystery Stories of 2019." Penzler shares editor credit with Johnathan Lethem.

Bourelle's story describes the lead character as "The Poet," who worked for "The Company" and "behaved like a man who didn't know he was being watched."

Another main character is "The Flame," a bilingual Spanish woman with "mahogany complexion and smooth dark hair that spilled down her shoulders," who also worked for "The Company."

The Poet was offered "retirement," which meant death, but not straight up assassination. Instead he was offered "The Gentleman's Exit or the Rogue's Exit. If you've been a good boy, you can be granted the Gentleman's Exit. This means they open three contracts. And they hire three other Gentlemen in your line of work to find you. You have one month. Thirty days. If you can evade — or eliminate — your competitors in that time, then you are free to go. You have earned your retirement….

No spoilers here, but I will say the fascinating story is spellbinding and unfolds with spectacular twists, gorgeous descriptions and dynamic action.

The attention Andrew Bourelle has brought to himself and Bold Venture Press is remarkable — a stream of new interest from readers hoping to learn more about pulp fiction magazines who have become collectors. And the mention in Penzler's book has also spurred submissions by writers who attempt to write "new pulp" hoping to get published.

Thanks Anderw Bourelle, Otto Penzler and Jonathan Lethem for creating interest in pulp fiction. ∎

HOME FOR KILLERS

A man can run just so far before he has to turn and face the devil that pursues him....

By
CHARLES BOECKMAN, JR.

AFTER I passed Goliad, the road turned to rutted clay. Thickets of blooming huisatche, cleared patches blanketed with blue-bonnets, chaparral clumps and now and then a freshly plowed field bordered the road. The wild, rolling Texas countryside spread around me like a giant patchwork quilt tossed out to soak up the spring sunshine.

The bitterness of years past came up into my mouth, as dry and acrid as the powdery white dust that curled around the tires of my canary-hued Buick convertible. I rested my fingertips on the steering wheel, half closing my eyes. The sunshine was good. I couldn't get enough of it. I wanted it to reach inside and warm the coldness that came to a man who'd been dead inside for a long time.

I swung off the road and down a narrow, barb-wire fringed lane, followed it for a mile, and pulled up at the farmhouse.

This is it, Joe Jureski. Your home. Remember? But, no, you wouldn't. That was too long ago to remember. A million years ago.

It hadn't changed much. It still needed a coat of paint. The porch roof sagged a little more, the barn leaned a bit more to the right. But the north forty had been broken into rich, moist loam, and the cattle grazing in the pasture were sleek. That would be Tom's doing. He would make a good farmer. It was in his blood, inherited from his father. I was grateful for that.

The sagging house dozed peacefully amidst its fields and cattle. Far up on a distant hill, the old moss-covered Spanish mission, La Bahia, brooded solemnly, like a tired old. sentinel guarding the countryside while reminiscing over its bloody past. Two buzzards wheeled in the clear blue sky." Somewhere a windmill creaked and a dog yelped.

She would have liked this, Joe. This warmth and peace and quiet. She'd never seen anything like this. Only gray city canyons and slum apartments and standing behind department store counters. That's why she looked so thin and pale and her eyes were so enormous.

But she's going to die, Joe. Because of you. So she won't get to see anything like this. Never ....

I WAS pounding my fist on the steering wheel, slowly, steadily, when a voice beside the car jerked me back to reality.

"Joe?" the voice murmured hesitantly, incredulously. I stared at the unruly-haired young man in overalls. He ran his wide-eyed gaze from one end of my sparkling pile of chrome and yellow metal to the other, then looked at me again and blinked.

"Tom!" I choked. I got out and hugged the kid, knocking his hoe out of his hand.

He was laughing and crying at the same time and saying my name over and over.

"You've come home from New York!"

I looked at him again. "I don't believe it, kid," I murmured softly, shaking my head. "When I left you were a youngster; now you're a man. But the place is hardly changed—looks wonderful to me."

"I've been running the farm, Joe," he told me proudly. "Since Dad—"

I nodded and looked down at my dust-covered imported tan shoes. "I was sorry, kid."

"We … The money you sent, Joe, covered all his funeral expenses. We were so glad. There wasn't any insurance."

"Forget it," I said roughly. I remembered that that had been back when I had the idea you could buy off your conscience. Now I knew differently. "I wanted to come for the funeral, Tom. I really did, but I just couldn't make it."

"Sure, Joe. We understood. New York is a long way off."

"Yeah," I said, and the word was like dust in my mouth.

He looked at the car again, admiringly. "You sure done well in New York, Joe. Real well!"

"Where's Ma?"

"In the house. But go easy, Joe. Her heart ain't so good anymore."

I went in and the smells and sounds swirled around me like ghosts out of the past. The twang of the patched screen door, fresh bread baking out in the kitchen, a kitten mewing. I moved into the dark parlor and my eyes picked out the plush sofa, the embroidered "Home Sweet Home" motto on the wall, the white blur that was the big seashell I used to hold to my ear.

She was sitting beside a window, looking through the family album at pictures and tokens of other days, her' lips moving silently. She looked up, and the lace curtain stirred and swirled around her.

The lines had furrowed deeply now, and her hair was like snow. Her eyes were faded, as if too many tears had washed the blue out of them. Her fingers trembled. "Joe!" she whispered.

I knelt beside her and she murmured something in Polish and cried.

"It's all right, Ma," I said. "I'm home now. To stay."

I WAS OUT in the barn, later, when I saw my sister, Pola. Tom had proudly taken me on a tour of inspection, showing me the silos bulging with feed, the sleek cattle, the chickens and the new farm station wagon. Pola, he'd said, was over at our neighbors.

He'd left me for a while and I was standing in the barn, chewing on a bit of straw, running my eyes over the harness and gear which was neatly mended and hung on the wall, when I heard a footstep behind me.

Years of instinctive training spun me around, whipped my hand up to the bulge under my coat. Then cold sweat washed my body and the strength went out of my knees and I clutched at a post.

"Mary," I gasped in a strangled throat. "Mary ...."

The pale, dark girl moved through the shadows, up close to me, frowning up at me, and then smiling. "Joe? Joe, don't you know me? Your sister?"

"Pola," I whispered. "Pola, darling!" In the dark barn, it was no wonder that I had for an instant mistaken her for Mary. She wasn't a little girl anymore. She was tall and slender, with wild, Slavic beauty, fully ripened. Her hair was like midnight, skin like fresh cream, a red, wide mouth, huge black eyes; her body was curved and soft and suddenly mature^

"Pola," I said. "You're beautiful!" She laughed, a little tinkling, silvery sound, and she kissed me. I knew it wasn't the first time a man had told her she was beautiful.

"Who did you mistake me for, Joe? One of your New York cuties?"

I took a cigarette, my fingers shaking. "Yeah," I said, with my mouth full of rags. "Yeah."

"Give me one of your cigarettes, Joe."

I handed her one. "Ma know you smoke?"

She shrugged, pouted a little as she leaned toward the lighted match I held. "A girl grows up some time, Joe. But parents don't think so."

She looked up at me and I noticed for the first time the violet smudges under her eyes, the tight lines around her mouth, the faint jaunted shadows in her black eyes. "Joe," she whispered with a strange, sudden intensity. "I'm glad you're back!"

Then she was laughing again. "There's a dance tonight, Joe. A real old-fashioned Texas country dance. You can see all your old friends. You can drive that nice yellow car and show everybody what a smart, rich brother Pola Jureski has!"

But her voice had little edges in it and the cigarette trembled between her fingers. She reminded me again of the girl in New York who had been afraid, too.

WE ALL dressed for the dance that night and I felt like a little kid again, washing behind my ears for Saturday night excitement. We took turns using the tin bathtub and Ma heated water on the iron cook stove and brought it in great steaming kettles. Pola and Tom fought over who'd get the bathroom when I was through with it.

In the bed-room, I dressed in a hundred-and-fifty-dollar imported plaid sport coat, a silk shirt, white and tan shoes. I knotted a sporty panel bow tie and looked in the mirror. There was a difference between Tom's lean, ruddy face and mine. Mine had pads of Soft flesh and a network of lines from too much rich food and liquor and soft, easy living.

Ma came in and sat on my bed. "So much fine clothes," she said, shaking her head. "So much money. It ain't my Joe. It's like I'm with a stranger."

I sat on the bed, took her frail hands in mine. "Ma, it's Joe. Your Joe, like always. You want to tell me something?"

She plucked at the home-made quilt, then smoothed her hands over her dress and gazed down at them. "It's Pola, Joe."

"Tell me about Pola, Ma. Is there something wrong? She looks worried, frightened."

Ma shook her head. "Too much beauty can be a curse, Joe. This boy she goes with. I don't know. I'm an old woman from a foreign country. I don't understand the ways

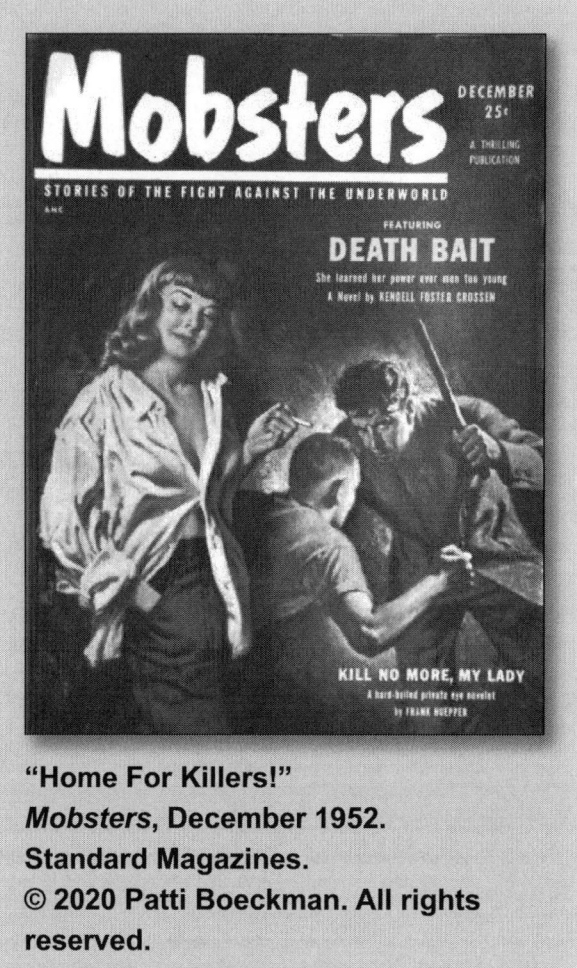

"Home For Killers!"
Mobsters, December 1952.
Standard Magazines.
© 2020 Patti Boeckman. All rights reserved.

of these young people. But they stay out so late, almost until morning. This boy doesn't work, but he's always got money." She shivered. "You tell me, Joe. You look at him close and tell me. You're smart, you know about these things. You look at him and tell me I'm a foolish old woman filled with fears for a too-pretty daughter."

She touched my cheek and whispered to me in Polish ….

I met Ralph Jessep. Pola introduced us when I went into the parlor. I looked at his quick, shifting eyes, his soft, manicured hands and his clothes that were too casually perfect and listened to his hard, bright talk. I knew why Ma was worried.

He shook hands with me, his eyes narrowing as if he sensed a kind of kinship between us. He was in his late twenties, a good ten years older than Pola. A blond man, fairly tall and well built, he had too much grease on his hair. But he would, I supposed, be considered handsome by a woman. Especially by a kid like Pola who'd lived on a farm and suddenly grown up and got her eyes full of Stardust.

Pola chattered brightly—too brightly. Her cheeks were flushed and her eyes glittered feverishly. But when her fingers brushed my hand, they were like ice.

"We'll see you at the dance, Joe, Tom. And don't you dare forget to dance with your sister!"

"I'll save them all for you, kid," I called after her. But there was a new coldness inside me. I stopped in my bedroom and strapped on the shoulder holster, which I'd first planned to leave in my bag.

Tom was taking the station wagon. He had a date with a girl in town. I kissed Ma and drove to the dance in the yellow convertible.

THERE seemed to be a thousand cars parked around the dancehall. It wasn't much of a town. Just a cotton gin and a general store and a huge, barn-like dancehall at the intersection of several country lanes.

The hall looked as big as an airplane hangar. A round structure with a tin roof, it had great wooden shutters on hinges all the way around that were propped open in summer so it became a cool pavilion. In front, under dangling lights, were the cold beer and soda stands. Here the older men lounged, talking crops and weather over cold beer and hamburgers.

I walked down there and I had a beer with the men who had been my father's neighbors. They remembered me as a teenage youngster, always in trouble at the community school.

When the music started, I bought a ticket and went into the hall. The floor was a great, round circle of polished hardwood, generously sprinkled with powder. The band sat on a raised dais on the far side. Long benches circled the floor behind a railing. Spectators would fill these as the crowd came in. And I knew that by midnight they would be littered with sleeping infants.

I drifted through the dancers and joined the crowd of stags in the center of the floor. The band—a piano, fiddle, guitar, drums, trumpet and clarinet—played the kind of rhythms I hadn't heard in a million years.

Schottisches, polkas, square dances and waltzes.

I couldn't find Pola anywhere among the dancers. The crowd drifted in from the parked cars until the dance floor was jammed with laughing, sweating humanity. I looked at my platinum wristwatch. It was nearly eleven before I saw her.

I followed her around the floor with my eyes until the band played a waltz. Then I cut in on her. "Hello," I smiled. "Remember me?"

Her dark eyes lifted to my face and her lovely red mouth twisted into a smile. "Yes, you're my brother Joe. My big brother who went away to New York and came back with a million dollars. Are you having a good time, Joe?"

I shook her firmly. "Pola, what's the matter? You're shivering."

The smile stayed on her face. It was fixed there. "Yes? I shouldn't be doing that. Should I, Joe? It's so warm." She bit down on a corner of her lip. "Joe, lend me the keys to your car. Just for a few minutes. No, please don't ask me why."

I stood there in the swirling crowd and watched her disappear. Then I cursed myself for many things and I pushed after her. By the time I bad worked through the crowd she was gone. I ran down through the parked cars. I heard a motor roaring. I saw the sweep of a long yellow convertible glittering with chrome bounce over a cattle guard and disappear down the dark road in a cloud of dust.

I RAN DOWN the line of parked cars, skinning my legs on fenders and bumpers until I found Tom's station wagon. I breathed a prayer of gratitude when I saw the keys in the ignition lock. I was out of the parking lot in seconds, leaving some dented fenders behind me. Then I was on the road behind Pola, eating her dust. I'd never catch her. That was out of the question. I could only follow her to where she was headed and pray that I didn't arrive too late.

Far behind me, I saw another car pull out of the parking lot. But I didn't think about that. I concentrated on not losing Pola.

When we struck the main highway, she veered to the right and I thought I knew then where she was heading. There was a town of about ten thousand population some twenty miles from here in that direction. On the straight highway, I lost her completely. I knew she was holding the convertible's speedometer near ninety. I tried not to think about that.

I didn't see the yellow car again until I crossed the railroad tracks on the outskirts of the town. I caught it out of the corner of my eye, parked in the shadows of the small, dark depot. I braked to a stop beside it, ran up the wooden stairs to the office.

Pola was sitting there alone, huddled on a bench away from the light.

See how much she looks like Mary, Joe ...

"Pola, honey ...." I sat beside her and I saw the train ticket clutched in her white fingers. Behind his cage, the white-haired old agent stared at us curiously.

She was crying without making a sound. "Please leave me alone, Joe. Go back to the farm with Tom and take care of Ma. Tell her I'll write soon."

I shook my head, holding her icy fingers. "It isn't any good, Pola, running away. You and I—we're alike. We always run. When we're afraid, we run."

"You've got to stay and face it, Pola, or you'll find you really didn't run away from what you were afraid of at all. You just made it worse."

I lit two cigarettes and gave her one. She dragged deeply on it, her cheeks hollowing. Then she let the smoke drift from her lips with a sigh, looking down at the cigarette between her enameled fingertips.

"It's Ralph Jessep, Joe. I didn't know it would be like this. He was so nice at first."

"You afraid of him—or something you did?"

"Him, Joe. After I'd been going with him a while, I found out he did all sorts of things. He gambles, steals. One night he held up a filling station while I was sitting out in the car. I cried all the way home, I was so scared. I told him I didn't want to see him again, ever. But he won't let me go. He threatens to do all sorts of terrible things to Ma. To Tom. He says he's crazy about me and I've got to marry him. Right away. Tonight."

The cigarette fell from her hand and she dug her long white fingers into her black hair. "I wouldn't care what he did to me, Joe," she sobbed. "But I'm afraid for Ma and Tom. I've got to go away. Far away."

"But you see, baby," I told her, "running wouldn't help. Ralph would find you, or he'd still be here if you came back. You don't solve things that way."

I ground my cigarette out under my heel, loosened the snub-nosed .38 automatic in my shoulder rig, and went out into the cool night. I thought that I knew now who'd been in the car that pulled out of the parking lot behind me back at the dance.

I LIT ANOTHER cigarette and stood there on the station platform, waiting. After a few minutes, a black sedan swung into the depot yard and parked beside the station wagon and my convertible.

I threw the cigarette away, walked down there before Ralph Jessep. got out.

I laid my hand on the door beside his shoulder. "Jessep, leave the kid alone. Beat it. She doesn't want to have anything to do with you anymore."

To make sure he understood, I jerked the door open and hauled the punk out and slapped him into the cinders. He crawled up, dragging at his hip pocket. He had his gun out before I could get to mine. He swung it across my face and a thousand stars exploded.

Far in the distance, I could hear him running. I dragged myself to my feet, swearing and shaking, my head to clear it. My mouth was full of blood and broken teeth.

I brought my gun up and split the night open. He stumbled, turned and fired. A coal raked my side. I doubled with a grunt, then got my balance ar:l followed him up on the platform. Somewhere in the distant pounding surf that filled my ears, I heard Pola scream.

Desperately I jogged down to the end of the platform, bent over from the fire in my side. I saw that he had Pola, was dragging her after him by her wrist. I couldn't risk another shot.

He'd jumped from the platform to a string of old freight cars, was running along their tops, forcing Pola to go with him. I could see that he planned to run down to the end until they were lost in darkness, then trawl down to the tracks and double back to the car.

The train Pola had been waiting for was puffing into the yards and its headlight silhouetted Jes'sep and Pola momentarily. I fired a wild shot over their heads. Jessep twisted to answer. There was one- horrible moment when he seemed to hang there, one-foot dangling, swinging his arms in the air to regain his balance. I don't know if he or Pola screamed just before he fell. But when I got to Pola, she was still screaming hoarsely, digging her fingers into her hair, looking down where Jessep had fallen to the tracks under the wheels of the puffing passenger.

I slapped the hysterics out of her, got her down to the cars. I made her drive the station wagon and I followed in my car. I knew in a few minutes there would be police and questions. I couldn't afford that. They could ask Pola later, after I'd gone.

We left the station wagon at the dance and I drove slowly home in my convertible. Pola cried herself to sleep on my shoulder like a little girl. I lifted her gently and carried her into the house and laid her on her bed. She stirred once, but kept right on sleeping, with her fingers curled beside her cheek on the pillow.

I sat beside her in the darkness, beside the flushed girl in the crumpled, torn evening gown. A moonbeam slanted through the window and caressed her tear-stained cheek.

I thought that Mary would look a lot like this tonight. She would have cried herself to sleep, too. Only there wasn't any big brother to help her out. Mary didn't have anyone. Not anyone.

QUIETLY, I went into my bedroom. I taped up the flesh wound along my ribs, changed my blood-soaked shirt for a clean one. I threw my clothes back in my two suitcases, picked them up and stole through the house.

I paused at Ma's room. I went in for a moment. Just a last look. But as I turned to leave, she whispered, "Are you going without telling me good-by, Joey?"

"Ma," I said. I sat on the edge of the bed, my eyes stinging with something they hadn't known in years.

She touched my hand. "Now you're my Joey again. Not a stranger anymore."

"I'm scared, Ma," I said simply.

"Yes. That's why you came down here. That's why you ran away from New York."

"I'm like Pola," I went on. "When there's trouble, I get scared and run. I don't face it. I don't think. I've always been like that."

She smiled sadly in the darkness.

Outside, the old windmill creaked, a chicken on the roost stirred; down in the huisatche a mockingbird sang. I sat there in the dark, quiet farmhouse and told her the whole story. I knew it would be better for her to know all of it, now.

It hadn't been like I'd told them in my letters. There hadn't been any important job with a fancy office and my name on the door. I'd made money, a lot of it—hut not that way. I'd found there were ways you could skirt the edge of the law and make it faster, easier. The numbers racket, and others. I'd had my fingers in a lot of things, none of them clean.

I got caught at last in a mess. It didn't matter about the details. I turned state's evidence and got a five-year suspended sentence. It had been my first offense.

But I was on probation, you see. I had to get a regular job, report every month and be careful who I was seen with.

It went along all right. I was scared.

I didn't want to spend those five years behind bars.

Then one night, two weeks ago, I met Mary. I walked into this bar and I saw her sitting in a booth alone. She was a thin, dark, pretty kid, about Pola's age. Looked a lot like her. I bought her a drink. We started talking, went to some other bars.

I didn't give her my right name. After a few drinks, she started bawling and told me about the trouble she'd had with her husband. A big, tough guy, his favorite pastime was beating her up when he came home from work at night. Tonight, he'd given it to her good. She'd run off.

That should have been my cue to drop her like a hot coal. But what the hell. I liked the kid, and I was lonesome too. We had some more drinks, started enjoying ourselves. We got in the jam at this bar around midnight. A drunk picked a fight with me. He came at me with a bottle. Without, thinking, I pulled my gun, shot him in the arm.

I WASN'T supposed to be carrying a gun. To be caught with it would break my probation. But I knew some of the boys I'd dealt with were sore at me for turning state's evidence and clearing out of the deals we'd been in. I felt a lot safer packing the heater.

If the police picked me up for shooting the drunk in the saloon, they'd throw the five-year suspended sentence at me. They were just waiting for something like this.

So I ditched the girl and ran. ...

The next morning, I read the papers. Nothing in them about the saloon fight—but the girl was there, her face right on the front page. It seems her husband had been murdered about eleven o'clock last night. The neighbors said they were always fighting. Last night they battled violently. Then things got quiet. The police picked the girl up, wandering around the park early the next morning. They'd charged her with the murder.

She swore that she'd been at a bar with a guy who'd picked her up at the time her husband was killed. She gave them the false name I'd given her. Of course, they couldn't find anyone by that name. None of the bartenders would identify her for certain. They were only human. They weren't sticking their neck out for a dame they weren't sure about.

I was the only one in New York who could prove she hadn't killed her husband. I could give her an alibi. But if I did, I'd have to explain about every place we'd been. The police would check and they'd find out about the tavern shooting. It would be five years for me.

I'd kept telling myself it wasn't my neck. Let the girl get out of the mess herself. I didn't want to do a five-year stretch. I'd seen what that could do to a man. God, I didn't want to do five years.

"But I couldn't run away from Mary,

CHARLES BOECKMAN

Hardboiled in the City ...
... and the Old West!

Available from:
www.boldventurepress.com

Ma. She followed me right down here. I see her every time I close my eyes. They'll give her the electric chair if I don't go back. She keeps saying that to me."

I kissed Ma. "Now you take care of yourself. I'll be back in five years or so. This time to stay. I promise."

I went out into the cool night and threw my bags in the car. I drew a deep breath, tasting the perfume of wildflowers, freshly turned earth and dew-wet grass. I thought that when I came back, I might be bringing a new wife with me. I thought that Mary would like to live down here where the air was fresh and clean and you didn't have to be afraid.

Five years wouldn't be so long if you had that to look forward to .... ∎

CHARLES BOECKMAN (1908-2015) grew up in Texas, which lent authenticity to his western fiction. His career as a jazz musician provided unique inspiration for his mysteries. In the 1940s and 1950s, he contributed to pulps like *Action-Packed*  *Western* and *Famous Detective*, and digests such as *Manhunt* and *Guilty*.

Eventually, he led his own jazz band. His wife Patti was a fellow musician and writer. A few of her "Silhouette" novels were co-authored with him.

He authored a comprehensive history of jazz. In 2009, he was awarded a star in the South Texas Music Walk of Fame in Corpus Christi, Texas. See more of his fiction and his autobiography *Pulp Jazz* at www.boldventurepress.com.

Art: Ed Coutts

Thubway Tham's Baggage Check

by Johnston McCulley

Everyone's favorite pickpocket decided to visit his old home — but Detective Craddock saw an opportunity to snare his nemesis once and for all!

HE sat in one corner of the smoking compartment of the Pullman car, next to the window, and watched the flying landscape closely. In one hand he held a railroad timetable, and he glanced at it, and at his watch, as each station was passed. If the limited was on time, very well and good; but, if it happened to be a couple of minutes late at any particular point, he acted as if about to go in search of the conductor and demand an immediate explanation.

For he was going home!

He was a little man, and apparently nervous to a great degree. His nostrils were thin, and his eyes furtive, and it seemed that his fingers were continually moving. Those same fingers were clever, though the other men in the smoking room did not guess it. Those fingers had been trained through the years, to explore foreign pockets quickly and without discovery.

But their owner had no intention of making them do their regular work now. The men in the smoking room with him, even had they been aware of his identity and reputation, could have continued their journeys without fear, and without keeping their hands on their wallets and watches continually. Those fingers, as a usual thing, did their nefarious work only in a certain small section of the vast country—a section toward which the limited now was rushing.

The little man who sat next the window in the smoking room had almost fought at Chicago to get an upper berth in an extra-fare train. He wanted to get to New York as quickly as possible, he had explained, hinting that it was a matter of life and death or something like that and even the extra-fare limited would be too slow. He had obtained the reservation—and now he sat at the window and watched the stations and the timetable, and fumed and fussed.

He made no attempt to hold a conversation with any of the other passengers in the smoking room, and if a man addressed him he got only a grunt by way of reply. The little man sitting next the window appeared to be occupied with his thoughts—which was exactly the case.

Down the river rushed the train, through city after city, devouring the miles with a speed that was amazing. Now it passed within a short distance of a great gray prison, whereupon the little man sitting next the window seemed to be trying to make himself yet smaller, and he almost closed his eyes.

He knew that prison well—he had spent a terrible three years there some time before. He shuddered at the memory of those three years.

He watched the sparkling river through the window. He began to notice things that he recognized and knew. His heart was warming gradually. He was getting home!

He had been away with the exception of one flying visit to the city, for a little more than a year, had been to the Pacific coast, had spent the greater part of the time in southern California, where the warm sunshine and soft sea breezes had done much for him.

He had been glad to make the journey to the Western country, for the state of his health had demanded an instant change of climate—and there had been other important reasons. But recently the great city on the Hudson had been calling him again, and finally he had packed his trunk and had answered the call.

The train was entering the outskirts of the city now, and the little man sat up straighter in his seat and betrayed a sudden interest. This was New York! This was home! She had her faults, but in all the world there was no other city like her! She could be cruel, and she could be kind. She was vast in some things, and small in others.

The little man left the smoking room and went into the car. He stopped beside his seat, put on his coat and hat and picked up his traveling bag.

"You gettin' off at Hundred an' Twenty-fifth?" the porter asked.

"I am!" the little man grunted.

The porter took the bag and started toward the end of the car, and the little man followed. He did not care to continue downtown to the Grand Central Terminal. He was not eager to have certain persons know that he had returned to the city—at least not until he had had an opportunity to see how things were going and learn any news that might have a peculiar interest for him. And at the Grand Central Terminal, he knew, there might be certain men who would recognize him instantly, and draw their own conclusions.

When the train stopped at the uptown station, he dropped off, hurried to the street; and walked along it rapidly for a distance of a few blocks. He came to a subway station—and stopped.

He dropped the bag to the walk and wiped the perspiration from his forehead. He looked around at the people and the signs and the buildings and at the subway station again. And then he grinned after the manner of a man who is well pleased.

"Thame old thubway!" he exclaimed. "Thame old plathe! It thertainly lookth good to me!"

And so Thubway Tham— What? You

didn't guess that it was Thubway Tham?

You know Thubway Tham, of course, the clever little pickpocket who worked only in the subway during rush hours—so clever that a city detective had been assigned especially to trail him.

You remember, perhaps, how Thubway Tham outwitted certain gentlemen with considerable profit to himself—one of the gentlemen being Craddock, the detective mentioned—and then went West for his health?

Now he had returned, benefited in every way, refreshed and more clever than before, his wits on keener edge. He stood before the subway station, and his nostrils opened wide to drink in the breath of the big tube he loved.

Thubway Tham was home!

He stood on the corner for as much as ten minutes, just enjoying the scene. Then he picked up his traveling bag, and hurried forward to purchase a ticket and start downtown.

II

Thubway Tham did not go to the rooming house where he formerly had lived. He knew that the place was under police surveillance, and he did not care, just at present, to let Craddock, his old enemy, know that he had returned.

He went to a small, respectable place and obtained a room. He ate a meal at an obscure restaurant, purchased the evening newspapers, and returned to his room to investigate the news.

He found something to interest him on the front page of his favorite journal. The article said that a certain broker of prominence, traveling in the subway because of a broken motor car, had been relieved of a wallet containing a large sum of money. The police, the article said, were of the opinion that there was a new subway pickpocket at work. They hinted that formerly there had been a famous pickpocket who worked in the subway, but that he had been out of the city for several months, hence could not be guilty of this latest crime. And there had been minor robberies recently, too, the newspaper said.

"Thome thilly thimp!" Thubway Tham told himself. "Playin' my game, ith he?"

And then a thought came to Thubway Tham.

He was believed to be out of the city. The detectives were searching for a new man—they were not looking for Thubway Tham. Why could not Thubway Tham do his work and let this new man, who had invaded a precinct sacred to Tham, take the blame for all the crimes? He could do it, Tham decided, as long as he kept from Craddock and others on the police force the knowledge that he had returned to the city.

Tham considered the matter throughout the evening, remaining in his room. He had told the landlord that he had just arrived from a long journey, was tired, and needed a long sleep. Tham realized that his appearance was not much altered, except that his cheeks were fuller and had a better color, and his hair was longer. His clothes were different, of course, but he couldn't place much faith in that fact. There was a slight risk he would have to run. He arose at an early hour the following morning, and after eating breakfast wandered around the streets, making friends with the great city

Originally Published In
Detective Story Magazine,
March 25, 1919.
Street & Smith Publications.

dock fought fair, at least.

"The old thilly ath!" Thubway Tham told himself. "Like to get a look at him juth to thee how he ith lookin'."

The rush hour came, and Thubway Tham descended into the subway at City Hall and started northward. He left the train at Times Square, and he took a fat wallet with him. Tham was glad to find that his fingers had not lost their cunning. He had been away for a year, and he had not worked at his "trade" during that time.

He boarded a train for downtown, and managed to get another wallet. He disposed of the "leathers" quickly, keeping only currency; which is very difficult to identify, especially if the bills are of small denominations.

He went back to Times Square, boarded the shuttle train, journeyed to Grand Central in the midst of the throng, returned, and lifted another wallet. Next he made the trip downtown again, went to his room, and found that the day's work had netted him a profit of about three hundred dollars. It was a far larger profit than usual. Thubway Tham considered it a good omen.

The morning newspapers were filled with articles about the carnival of crime in the subway, and certain detectives received orders that something had to be done or there would be divers and sundry transfers and things like that.

Once more, Thubway Tham worked at rush hour. He worked carefully, yet desperately. In the old days he had been content to lift one wallet, or perhaps two at the most, but that was when Craddock was trailing him most of the time and he was obliged to work beneath the nose of the

again. He did not visit any of his old haunts, however, and he was alert for detectives who might recognize him. He wanted to see and talk to his old friends, but he knew that it would not do at present.

Word soon would be spread around town that Thubway Tham had returned, and it would reach the ears of the police, and Craddock.

Tham wondered a great deal about Craddock.

There had been quite a fight between them in the old days—a game of wits in which Tham always had emerged the victor. Craddock had sworn to "get him," but Crad-

detective.

Now he lifted wallets as rapidly as possible, for he wanted to maintain the carnival of crime.

Reports poured into police headquarters, and a superior officer in the detective department sent for Craddock.

"Something funny about this subway business," he said.

"It's either a new man—or a gang," Craddock replied.

"Looks like a gang, the number of reports we've been getting. How about Thubway Tham?"

"Still out of town," Craddock said. "I got to thinking about him, too. I've trailed around his old hangouts, but haven't found a trace of him. Been expecting him to come back about this time, and have been watching for him. If he was back, he'd show himself right away. He'd think it was smart to dare me to catch him."

"Well, get busy!" Craddock's superior warned him. "I don't like this chorus of howls. We've got to land somebody, and do it mighty quick. Get busy!"

Craddock and his associates got busy. They haunted the subway from one end of it to the other.

They rode back and forth until they began to hate the underground railroad, yet they caught no pickpockets, either male or female.

Thubway Tham, reading the newspapers carefully, knew that he was not the only man working in the subway. There were reported robberies of which he had not been guilty.

Wherefore rage was born within him.

In the old days, before he had gone west, it had been understood in the underworld that Thubway Tham's district was the big tube, and other dips refrained from working there. Once a man had tried it, and Thubway Tham had punished him. Here was somebody trying it now.

But Tham was honest in his way. He had not let it be known in the underworld that he had returned, and so he could not exactly blame the man who was working in his district. He was not ready yet to let anybody know he was in the city.

For a week, he worked during the rush hours.

He obtained many wallets, and at the same time he watched for the other man, but never located him.

Tham was piling up money, but he knew that it could not go on. Half a dozen times he had narrowly escaped being seen by an officer who knew him. And, if he was recognized, the people at headquarters might blame all the recent subway work on him!

"I thuppothe I'll have to let 'em know that I am in the thity thoon," Tham told himself one evening.

"Then that ath of a Craddock will be on my trail.

He'll pether the life out of me! There ith no uthe talkin'—thometimeth that man maketh me thick!"

The following day, he saw Craddock at a distance, but managed to prevent himself being observed by the detective. And, half an hour later, on an express train approaching Fourteenth Street, Thubway Tham found his rival.

He saw the man do his work—take a wallet from a fat individual who carried it in his hip pocket. When the dip left the train, Tham followed.

The other man was tall and broad-shouldered, and did not look at all like the ordinary pickpocket, a fact that probably had saved him from arrest, he had the appearance of an ordinary businessman. "Thilly ath!" Tham said. "Workin' my game, ith he? I'll get thquare with him!"

He followed his rival into the subway again at another station, watched him lift another leather, and edge forward. Tham waited his chance, until the other was about to leave the train at a crowded platform. His hand made a lightning-like movement—and Tham had the wallet the other man had stolen. He remained on the train as his rival left, and he was smiling.

That night, as he sat in his room, he began considering that it perhaps would be better, now, to visit his old haunts. If Craddock met him, and learned that he had been in the city for some days, the detective would believe he had been hard at work. Tham wanted Craddock to keep on looking for a criminal who was a stranger. He even wanted Craddock to take that stranger into custody after a time, for Tham felt sure that the other man was an outsider who had no business robbing the people of New York.

On the following day, Tham went forth as usual, alert for officers of the law, ready to dodge any old friend he might see, eager to make a last haul before announcing his presence in the city.

He boarded a train at Union Square and started uptown. At the next station, he saw his rival get aboard.

Thubway Tham had noticed a prosperous looking gentleman standing near one end of the car, and had speculated on removing valuables from the gentleman's pocket. But now he watched his rival.

The tall man glanced at the others in the car, and he, too, saw the prosperous-looking individual.

Thubway Tham realized that the other had picked this man for a victim, and he felt his anger gathering again. With all the subway trains, and with all the persons riding on them, was it at all necessary for this interloper to pick the man that Tham himself had decided to rob?

"Maketh me thick!" Tham growled low down in his throat.

He decided to allow the tall man to work his will. Something like a hunch had come to Thubway Tham. He had a feeling of uneasiness. There seemed to be disaster in the air. He made his way toward the other end of the car, but got into a position from which he could watch the other.

The train was approaching a station. Tham saw the other man's hand make a familiar move, and turned away. Instantly he turned back again—for to his ears had come a screech of rage.

The rival pickpocket had bungled. His victim had caught him in the act. Now they were scuffling at the other end of the car. Thubway Tham saw that the tall man could not get rid of the wallet he had taken. And then another man took a hand in the game—a broad-shouldered, black-mustached man Tham knew instantly for an officer working in plain clothes.

The train stopped at the station, and officer, prisoner and victim got off. Tham rode to the next station and then returned downtown by means of the back streets.

The thing had unnerved him to a degree.

III

Thubway Tham did no work for the following week, and he spent a great deal of time in his room.

The papers announced the capture of the pickpocket, and that the carnival of crime in the subway apparently had come to an end. That was what Thubway Tham wanted. He grinned when be read that the prisoner disclaimed knowledge of more than half the recent robberies. The police did not believe him, of course, especially since the crimes had ceased with his arrest.

At the end of the week, Tham considered that it now would be safe for him to enter the city officially and make his presence known. That would be the best way, he knew. He could not hope to hide, and if caught doing it, he merely would cause Craddock and the others to suspect him and watch him more than usual.

He went far uptown one morning, and for a time walked around Central Park. It was his last chance for some time, he knew. Craddock had told him more than a year and a half before that his presence in that section of the city would mean instant arrest on a vagrancy charge. Men of Thubway Tham's ilk knew better than to invade certain parts of the metropolis.

He sat down on a bench behind a clump of brush, in a secluded part of the park, and gave himself up to meditation. After a time, voices reached his ears, and he realized that two men were on the other side of the clump of brush, and that they were speaking in low tones.

Thubway Tham parted the bushes and observed them. They were well dressed and appeared to be persons of prominence, but Tham knew instantly that they were not honest men.

"Amateur crookth," he told himself.

Tham hated an amateur crook. The underworld hated them. Genuine crooks, who knew the ethics of their calling, were all right. They played the game, and if they were caught they paid the penalty.

Either a crook or an honest man, but not an attempt to be both, said the underworld.

Thubway Tham grew interested in the conversation he heard, and in what he saw. One of the men opened a traveling bag he had, took several packages of bills from his pocket and put them into the bag. The other watched for anybody to approach.

"Now we'll go to the Grand Central and check this bag," one of the men was saying. "That's the safest thing in the world. We'll leave it there until the investigation is over at the office. When we are sure that they do not suspect us, we'll merely take down the check, pay the storage bill, and catch a train."

There was considerably more talk, and Thubway Tham drank it in. It appeared that these men had robbed an employer who believed them to be faithful. They had worked for him for years; and had decided to take all they could at one time and depart for other scenes.

"Why, the dirty crookth!" Thubway Tham told himself.

The men walked on through the park, and Tham followed them at a distance. Had these been genuine, professional crooks, he would have turned away from them, but an amateur crook was to be despised and taught the error of his ways when possible.

Tham followed them to the nearest subway entrance, and got on a train behind them. He was alert for sight of an officer, glad that he saw none.

The Grand Central was dangerous territory, he knew. There always were detectives prowling around the big station.

The men went to the check stand, and one of them checked the bag and put the pasteboard into a pocket of his waistcoat. Then they left the station and started walking along Forty-second Street.

Thubway Tham trailed them through the crowds, trying to keep them in sight constantly and dodge officers at the same time. Now and then he got near enough to realize that they were maintaining a conversation, but he could not distinguish their words.

He followed them to Times Square and down into the subway. They boarded an express for downtown, and Thubway Tham got into the same car with them.

Tham wanted that check, but taking a thing like that from a waistcoat pocket is dangerous and requires a maximum of skill. Assured that no officer he knew was in the car, he worked near the two men, who were standing, and finally was pressing against the one who had the check.

Thubway Tham began to despair. He watched for an opportunity, but none presented itself. Then accident came to his aid.

At one end of the car, one man stepped upon the foot of another. The apology was not accepted, and hot words followed. There was a sudden commotion as fisticuffs started, and the man who had the check in his pocket stretched his neck and bent his head to see the row. Thubway Tham's hand did its work, and the check was in his possession.

He left the train at the next station, and immediately caught another uptown. He reached Times Square, took the shuttle to Grand Central, and hurried toward the parcel check stand. And then he saw his old enemy, Detective Craddock.

Tham dodged behind half a dozen persons who were crowding forward to the stand, He saw another detective, and dodged back. Craddock caught sight of him, hurried toward him.

"Well, well, if it isn't my old friend Tham!" Craddock said.

Tham regarded him with scorn. "By heaventh!" said Tham. "I no thooner get back to town than I am pethered with the thight of your homely fathe! I went away and thtayed a whole year jutht to forget your ugly mug, and here you are waitin' when I come back."

"Just in from the Golden West, eh?"

"The Wetht may be golden, but little old New York ith good enough for me," Tham said.

"Well, I suppose you'll be up to your old tricks again, Tham," Craddock told him. "I suppose I'll have to trail you as I did before, to keep you from bothering gentlemen with wallets."

"Thay! Jutht becauth I onthe wath thent up—"

"Now, please don't begin that, Tham. Don't start any of that 'give a dog a bad name' stuff on me. I'm wise to you, Tham, all right, and don't you forget it!"

"Withe? You?" Thubway Tham sneered. "If you are withe, I mutht be King Tholomon himthelf. If you are withe I am a college profethor. If you are withe—"

"Pray, cease!" Craddock said. "When did you get in?"

"Thith morning," Tham replied, remembering that there was a morning train from Chicago that was a favorite with the traveling public.

"Sure of that?"

"Of courthe. Why?"

"Tham, somebody has been working your beat."

"What do you mean by that?" Tham demanded.

"I mean that, up to a week or so ago, some gent has been bothering persons in the old subway. He picked pockets right and left and center, Tham. But we got him."

"Tho?"

"Caught him with the goods, Tham; and that's what we're going to do to you one of these days if you don't change your mode of life. And this particular crook declares he didn't commit half those crimes Tham. Some of them seemed a lot like your work. If I thought you had been in town any length of time, I'd just take you up to talk to the captain about it."

"Well, my grathiouth!" Tham exclaimed. "I don't any more than get off the train before I am accuthed of thomething! Before I get a chance to rent me a room—"

"You're quite sure you just got in this morning, Tham?"

"Of courthe!"

"And you haven't rented a room yet?"

"No. I am going to my old plathe, if you want to know."

"Then, where is your bag?" Craddock demanded, pointing a finger at him. Thubway Tham gulped. He had been afraid of that question, but he was ready for it.

"In the check thtand," he replied. "Here ith the check. Thee? You make me thick, Craddock!"

Thubway Tham turned his back, went to the stand, and handed in the check. To say that he felt no fear would be to write a falsehood. He was desperately afraid that Craddock would insist that he open the bag. And how could he, when he had no key for it? If it was opened, how could he explain those packages of money and the other articles?

He was glad that his back was turned toward Craddock, for it gave him time to compose himself.

The bag was handed to him, and he whirled around again, a smile on his face.

"It ith good to be back, even if your ugly fathe ith the firth I thee," Thubway Tham said. "Will you hold thith bag, Craddock, while I light a thigarette?"

Detective Craddock would, and did. He carried the bag, moreover, as they walked to the main entrance, for it seemed that Thubway Tham had trouble with his matches.

"Going to use the subway?" Craddock asked.

"Of courthe!"

"Um! I guess I'll just ride a part of the way with you, Tham."

"Go ath far ath you like," Tham told him. "We thtrive to pleathe. I am goin' to

(Continued on page 131)

It was a challenge Bill couldn't ignore. His mortal enemy had dared him to combat in that space more than five astronomical units from earth. Though he knew his weapons were far inferior, he knew, too, that Sparling had in his power the girl Bill loved

Bill reached up and grabbed a fin of his ship. They had won!

SPACE BURIAL

By LEW MERRILL

BILL SPARLING, roused from his well-earned nap by the shout of Vulcan, his Martian aide, went forward to the wheel of the little Jonesing spaceship. Putting his eyes to the refracting optoscope Bill could see a curious, elongated body some five hundred miles ahead.

He glanced at the dial of the Jonesite gravity tank. Plenty of gas to take him to Hungaria, the first of the outer planetoids. He thumbed the speed control, and saw the indicator drop to a thousand miles an hour — to five hundred — to a hundred and ten. That was as slow as he dared drive the old ark; anything under that would bring her within the gravitational field — not of Hungaria, but of menacing Jupiter. And many a better and stronger Jonesing ship had been wrecked by the terrific planet, dashed to destruction in the heart of its boiling mass.

The *Girl Unknown* was idling in space now. Bill watched the distant object, then looked at the gravitational equivalent dial. The needle was creeping up — that red thread whose approach to the black line meant danger. Once it crossed it, the anti-gravitational force would be less than Jupiter's attraction. Bill increased his speed to a hundred and thirty, and the red line remained stationary, began to recede. The elongated body was coming plainly into view.

"Is a man!" shouted Vulcan. No Martian could use the explosive, tongue-to-palate sound of "t."

It was the body of a man. Bill watched in amazement as the *Girl Unknown* moved toward it. Then a cry broke from his lips. He recognized that face, with the shock of snow-white hair, the straggling white beard, even though the habitual black clothing had been stripped off and the corpse flung to destruction in its thermotex underwear.

It was the body of old Houghton, the missionary on the Hilda group of planetoids, beyond the gap that separated them from Eros and Hungaria. Everybody knew and loved Houghton. Even his enemies, of the nectarine trade, respected him, despite the fact that he was their bitter opponent in their nefarious business.

A last glance through the optoscope showed Bill the manner in which the old man had met his death. The top of the head had been crushed in by a ferocious blow.

Mechanically Bill's hand went to the grappler. The first cast hooked the body, and the mechanism drew it up through the void-locks inside the ship. Bill placed it on the long seat and looked at it, swallowing hard, thinking.

The body was not, of course, decomposed, in the absence of air and bacteria, though it was considerably desiccated, owing to the dissipation of the body fluids into space, so that it was becoming mummified. Probably Houghton had been dead about a week.

Bill's anxiety grew. If Houghton's enemies had got him, what about Ursula? When she was graduated from high school in New York she had insisted on rejoining her father at his headquarters on Hilda, where she had been born, and grew up. Bill, who had brought Houghton news of his daughter, and vice-versa, on his periodical visits, had joined the chorus that urged the girl to remain on earth. In a few years, Houghton's service would end, and the Board would pension him. Life on the planetoid Hilda offered nothing, except the company of her father.

One of the marvels of astronomical research had been the discovery that the major planetoids retained an atmosphere. But there had been only vegetative life on them, until their settlement by political exiles, two hundred years before:

These had quickly slipped into a state of white savagery, existing on the groundfruits that were plentiful on all the planetoids. They had been forgotten during the century of civil wars on Earth. And now they had come into prominence because of the illicit "nectarine" trade.

Because the population of Earth, now numbering no more than a million, had almost ceased to reproduce itself, owing to inbreeding, a score of governments welcomed the introduction of fresh blood in the shape of planetoid girls, through whom the race could be rejuvenated. These were sold at fabulous prices. And the central government at New York had strictly forbidden the traffic, on account of the abuses to which it gave rise.

Despite the presence of space-cruisers, the surreptitious traffic in human flesh continued. Houghton had devoted most of his energies to helping suppress it. Now they had got him. And Bill Sparling could guess who was at the back of the dastardly murder.

His fears for Ursula grew. For she was the "Unknown Girl" after whom he had named his ship. A lucky strike of Jonesite, and he would be in a position to ask her to marry him.

IN SPITE of the development of anti-gravitational fields, which made possible journeys to the planets, these had always had a considerable element of danger in them until the discovery of Jonesite. And that had been the scientific sensation of its decade.

Among the innumerable particles that filled all known space, certain ones had been discovered that remained more or less stationary, instead of rushing on an erratic course at the rate of thousands of miles a minute. These were hard gray pellets which, analyzed, proved to be of osmonium, the heaviest of the elements, one of the uranium group.

And, like uranium, osmonium was constantly giving forth a radioactive property that had the unique effect of neutralizing gravitation.

The most valuable of the elements, osmonium could not be discovered in sufficient quantities.

Hence the vast fleets of Jonesing ships, plying among the planetoids, the staking out of claims, the violence and lawlessness among the crews, the rivalries, and battles.

Hungaria, the outermost planetoid, was pretty well policed. But the Hilda group, at a distance of 3.9 astronomical units, was the hunting-ground of the Jonesing ships, which were not averse from a little nectarining on the side. Past solitary Thule were the six of the Trojan group, at 5.2 units' distance from Earth, and here even the space-cruisers did not ply. For the six Trojans were too perilously close to the orbit of Jupiter when in alphelion.

Well, there was nothing to do but commit Houghton's body to its last repose. Bill wrapped a blanket about it, spoke the few words of the burial service that he could remember, went to the front, and took the wheel from Vulcan. A glance at the complicated direction chart above his head, a brief calculation, and he changed direction, set the speed control again. The ship leaped up to a thousand, two thousand, four thousand miles an hour.

"Huh! Ranger!" shouted Vulcan, shaking his wooly head. "Danger" was what Vulcan had meant to say. He pointed to the g.e. dial. The red thread was almost over the black needle.

"It's all right," said Bill. He stepped back and opened the void-locks. He took old Houghton's body in his arms and placed it in the cage. Soundlessly it slid into the void.

Bill changed direction for Hungaria. The red thread slipped back. He had driven the ship just close enough to the orbit of Jupiter to insure that Houghton's body would fall into the maw of the giant planet or join the ceaseless, innumerable procession of its satellites.

Space-burial! Well, it was a fitting end for the old missionary. But fear for Ursula, and black rage on account of her father's murder, tore at Bill's heart. He meant to pick up certain trails on Hungaria, principally that of Jeribald and his gang of Jonesiters and nectariners.

LI MOW'S was packed to overflowing, for Bill had arrived at the time of the semi-annual sale of Jonesite. It was crammed with the Chinese buyers who almost monopolized the trade. Several score of Jonesite fishers, whose ships lay moored in the air-harbor, were staggering about the group of buildings that comprised the bar, letting themselves go in drunken frenzy, fighting, quarreling, or drinking at the bar, and displaying fistfuls of the precious chunks to prospective purchasers.

The atmosphere on all the planetoids that possessed an atmosphere corresponded to that on Earth — had, in fact, been captured from Earth's moon and from Mars, scientists thought, through some principle not yet completely elucidated. The main difference was that a visitor to Hungaria had to wear half-ton shoes — containing a nucleus of matter under dwarf-star condensation — to keep from covering a thousand yards at every stride, on account of the slight gravitational attraction.

Stamping up toward the building, Bill heard titters from windows. Girls in extreme *deshabille* were leaning out, gesturing to him. Girls of any age from eighteen to thirty. Li Mow prided himself upon his *clientele*. Other space-houses might take the dregs and leavings of Earth, especially the "nectarines" who were trying to drift back to their planetoids — and seldom reached them. Li Mow was particular.

Earth, under her woman rulers, had taken all the joys out of life. Death for drinking, death for smoking, death for love outside the marital bond — which accounted for most of the bootleg love provided by the "nectarines." But even the captains of the space-cruisers winked at what went on upon Hungaria. You couldn't push human nature beyond a certain limit. Hungaria was the red-light district of the planetary system. It had to be, and the woman rulers had to wink at its existence too.

THERE fell a silence as Bill approached the long bar, and Bill read the confirmation of his worst fears in it. Jeribald was the most notorious nectariner among the planetoids. That wasn't Bill's business, but Jeribald and his men were suspected of having robbed and murdered one of Bill's friends.

A crude job. They had miscalculated their space-burial, so that the battered body had come floating down to the surface of Hungaria later. There was no proof. But Bill and Jeribald had been at odds ever since. This silence made Bill's heart hammer slowly and heavily. He was thinking of Ursula, alone on Hilda.

"Hello!" Li Mow greeted him, pushing forward a glass and bottle. "Velly glad to see you, Bill. You start for Jonesite glounds?"

"Where's Mr. Houghton?" demanded Bill abruptly. The old man used to hold a missionary meeting about the time of each sale; his old ship, scraped and battered by swarms of aerolites, between Hungaria and Hilda, was a space-mark.

"Not come yet," said Li Mow.

Bill looked about him, and saw that everybody present knew what had happened to Houghton, even the little dusky Martians, scurrying about with glasses.

"All ships not yet come, Lil Mow continued. "Jellibald ship not yet come. You bling Jonesite? You want to sell?"

"No, I've been on Earth the past season," said Bill. His mother was sick, had urged him to remain, but Bill wanted one more trip to a field he had discovered, where the Jonesite pellets were thick. Then he believed he could persuade Ursula to leave her father and try luck with him.

"I'll have plenty Jonesite for you when I come back," he said.

"Plices go down. You better hully," said Li Mow, and everybody laughed. "Jellibald find a new field, plenty Jonesite there. He no care if plice goes down. Beyond Hilda group, near Thule."

Now Bill understood, from the grinning faces about him. That was no doubt the field he had himself discovered. He had staked it out with flags and Jonesite beacons, a quadrangle in space fifty thousand square miles in extent that no tug of gravity could affect. Within that space, by law, all Jonesite pellets were his.

But Jeribald wasn't likely to respect his claim. Jeribald had Tuck, Garrou, and Blacky, the Martian, with him, three outstanding ruffians, and his ship carried a three-millimeter neutron gun, in flat defiance of the law against the arming of spaceships. She could smash anything except a space-cruiser.

HOT rage burned in Bill as he turned away, conscious of the covert sneers of everybody in Li Mow's. Out among the Hilda planetoids, where it was every man for himself, the will of the strongest man was law. Poor Danny Briggs had disputed that law, and his battered body, gravitating to Hungaria, had attested to it. Bill had been waiting to catch Jeribald ever since.

He let his hand close over his neutron pistol. The feel of it under his pultex gave him courage. He moved up the street toward the harbor, over which the lit boats moved like fireflies as they scurried between the small wharf and the ships at anchor. Again he heard the tittering of the girls at the windows. Then his name called:

"Bill! Bill Sparling!"

The girls knew him, of course, and always mocked him, because he would have nothing to do with them. But the sound of his name made him turn. He saw a woman's face hazily outlined under her robe in the light of the little solar lamp behind her.

"Come here, and I'll tell you what you want to know."

"What do I want to know?" Bill parried. But then he recognized the girl. Her name was Astra, and she had been nectarined to Earth in childhood. Jeribald had got possession of her, and brought her to Hungaria, used her as his intermediary in many shady transactions that concerned Jonesite. Also in matters political, since Hungaria was one of the military bastions of Earth. Whoever ruled Hungaria, was master of Earth, the proverb ran. Hence the presence

Art: H. J. Ward
Spicy-Adventure Stories,
February 1941.
Culture Publications, Inc.

of the space-cruisers, which were not among the planetoids solely to preserve order among the Jonesiters.

The girl disappeared. A handle clicked, a door slid back. The little solar light within shed a shaded glow over the room, with its sumptuous furniture. A rich, hand-woven rug covered the floor, a thinner one the divan, which was piled with pillows.

"I never thought that I should see you here, Bill Sparling," said Astra.

"Nor I you," answered Bill. "I thought that Jeribald always took you along with him on his trips to the Jonesite fields."

INSTEAD of answering, she flung back the silken robe that covered her. Beneath it was a short, gossamer-thin garment, spun of spider-silk, and flashing with all the colors of the spectrum as the solar light caught its shimmering folds. It fell from bosom to knee, but hid nothing of Astra's beauty. From the curve of the shapely shoulders, from the perfection of her small, firm breasts, to the tapering waist and the curving thighs ran streaks of opalescent flame.

Astra shook her head, and her heavy, red-gold hair tumbled in a cascade down her back. She extended two arms of alabaster, put her hands on Bill's shoulders.

"You've been so blind, Bill. I've loved you so long, and Jeribald kept me close when he had me in his ship."

She drew closer to him, and the perfume of her made Bill giddy; the warmth of her made his heart beat fast as her arms circled his neck.

"I've seen you often and I've always loved you, Bill. Jeribald guessed it. That's one of the reasons why he hates you. Kiss me, Bill, and I'll tell you what you want to know."

Her lips met his with crushing pressure, and the roundness of her breasts became a broken bar against his chest. Astra hadn't been a nectarine for nothing; she had been taught the arts of love in the infamous school on Hilda, against which poor old Houghton had fought so vainly.

Against such arts, Bill had as much chance as a kitten in the grip of a terrier. His head swam, and, grasping Astra in his arms, he swayed heavily toward the divan.

Astra's spider-silk underwear seemed

to melt into her body, which became a rippling, iridescent glow. Streaks of that opal fire traversed it as it strained itself against Bill in undulations that shot fire through all his arteries.

Then slowly the thought of Ursula came back to Bill, and whips of shame scourged him. He groaned, and heard Astra's tinkling laughter.

"Take me with you, Bill, and I will show you where she is," she said.

"Has Jeribald got her?"

"He said he was going to seize her and take her to his hideout in the Trojans."

"The Trojans? He can't venture there."

"His hideout is on Nestor. He has enough Jonesite to keep his ship from being drawn into Jupiter's orbit. But we may find him on the field you staked out near Hilda. He is seizing all the Jonesite there. You take me, and I'll show you."

"I — can't — take you."

"I am going to show Jeribald I don't care, because I have you now. If you don't take me, I won't show you his hideout on Nestor. I know just where it is; he has described it many times."

THERE wasn't any arguing with Astra, and it was no use telling her that he loved Ursula. The minds of the nectarines didn't look forward to the future in the way of Earth-minds. Astra meant to accompany Bill on his journey, and that was the end of it.

Taking a boat back to the *Girl Unknown* with Astra, Bill found Vulcan engaged in checking the fueling of Jonesite gas from the supply tender. The brief darkness had already given place to the subdued daylight on Hungaria. The sun, one-third the size that it appeared from Earth, was traversing the heavens in its swift course. Bill relieved Astra and himself of their half-ton shoes, and found another pultex suit for her, a perfect non-conductor of temperature, alike on the air-encircled asteroids and in airless space. He laid it out beside her, and set out a meal of Earth-baked bread and some tinned stuff.

He had set a course direct for Hilda. The *Girl Unknown* could outspeed Jeribald's more powerful but clumsier ship. If Jeribald was on the claim that he had staked out, Bill meant to anchor behind the rocks of Hilda and try to capture the larger boat by surprise. He didn't dare let his mind dwell on Ursula. He resigned himself to the long hours of waiting.

Astra snuggled up beside him. She had put off her robe in the hot compartment, and she was a nectarine girl, for whom life meant love. In the circle of her arms, and dazed by the shimmering undergarment, Bill was lost again.

Hours passed. Day and night followed each other at brief intervals. Sometimes Astra whispered to Bill of a life on Earth, after she had avenged herself on Jeribald for the trick he had played her. Sometimes Bill lay, sunk in exhaustive, gloomily anticipating the future, until Astra's white arms involved his senses again. He hated her in the intermissions of her embraces, and he couldn't see how he could manage to free himself from her.

Out of the lethargy that held him, Bill was aroused by a shout from Vulcan, who, like all Martians, slept only at intervals of two Earth-weeks, and had been sitting tirelessly at the controls.

Hilda, Mas'er! Hilda!" he called, raising his black face with the earnest, dog-like eyes, and wagging his stumpy tail.

Through the optoscope Bill could see the onrushing mass of the irregularly shaped planetoid. Hastily he scanned the heavens as they shot forward. There was no sign of Jeribald's space-ship.

"Anchor off the Mission!" Bill ordered the Martian.

Clad in their pultex, and wearing their heavy hoots, Bill and Astra disembarked on the rocky shore. The sight of the Mission appalled Bill. That was Jeribald's work all right. The pirate hadn't been content to kidnap and kill old Houghton; he had blasted the buildings of heavy stone to pieces with his neutron gun. On Earth such enormous masses heavier than the stones of the Pyramids, could hardly have been lifted save by hydraulic power, but on Hilda it had been a simple matter for Houghton to construct the Mission with his own hands.

The whole building was blasted to pieces, except for one corner, where, from beneath a crazily sagging roof, a dozen girls came trooping forward.

Wild girls, the descendants of the original exiles, nude save for the goassmer wisps of spider-web about their waists, for Hilda was hot during its brief day, and in winter, the denizens retreated into the underground caves that were a feature of the asteroid. All young, all exquisitely moulded, running forward to Bill with little cries of delight.

Their white bodies swayed, their small breasts oscillated as they clung to him, while Astra stood by in scowling silence.

"Where's Ursula?" Bill demanded. "The girl who lived here with the old man. Where is she?"

"Ka pesna hu ha sorkha," answered a big brunette, with a languishing look.

"She asks you to take them all away to Earth," Astra interpreted.

"Ask her where the girl is — Houghton's daughter."

There was a voluble interchange. "She says Jeribald took her away fifteen days ago, and he is coming back to take them all to Earth. She says they love you and want you to take them instead."

Fifteen days! But that meant fewer than two Earth-days. Bill grasped the girl again. "Where's Jeribald?" he shouted.

"She says," interpreted Astra, after another interchange, "that you will find out if you go to your Jonesite ground."

BILL hurled the *Unknown Girl* through space. The meteors thick about the Hilda group, battered her sides, gray chunks of Jonesite, aggregating a substantial sum in value, crashed against her duralloy sheathing. Bill had taken the ; Astra was curled up in the rear compartment; Vulcan, his time for sleep not yet arrived, watched his master with adoring eyes. Bill hurled the vessel forward until her engine quivered, and the sound of the mechanism, inaudible without, crackled and roared as it echoed through the hollow of the shell.

He was nearing his claim now, and constantly he gazed through the optoscope, looking for Jeribald's ship.

It had grown dark, and that darkness

seemed Bill's one hope. If he could creep up unobserved, and dodge the deadly neutron gun, he might grapple Jeribald's ship and board her, fight it out, he and Vulcan against Jeribald, Tuck, Garrou, and Blacky. A desperate chance, but not more desperate than leaving Ursula in the power of the man.

Still there was no sign of Jeribald's ship. But something loomed up at about a hundred miles' distance. It was one of Bill's Jonesite beacons, with the flag atop, a structure some fifty feet high by six inches in thickness — of course it would never topple without compelling gravity —composed of lumps of crude Jonesite sufficient to render it neutral despite the shifting attractions of the whirling asteroids.

When he was within a hundred miles, Bill saw a patch of red on the flag. He slowed the ship, looked at his g.e. dial. The red needle leaped toward the red. Bill had calculated the position of Jupiter. He had halted there to stake out his claim when the pull of the mighty planet was neutralized by the proximity of Hilda. Hilda was receding. It was a gamble Bill had to take. He stopped the engine, felt the ship rock and strain, flung out his grapnel through the little hand-lock and drew in the sheet of red papyroid, scored by the transverse passage of a dust-sized aerolite.

A challenge from Jeribald: "If you dare, Sparling, meet me on Nestor." And beneath it, "Love," and the name erased by the aerolite. But in Ursula's writing.

Astra was looking over Bill's shoulder. "You dare not go to the Trojan group. They're too near Jupiter. Turn back, Bill. Take me away."

"I'll follow Jeribald to hell," said Bill.

Astra clung to him. "I'm afraid, Bill. And you're afraid. You dare not go to the Trojans. You haven't power enough in your ship to try. Take me back to Earth, Bill."

Bill flung the pleading girl from him and settled himself at the controls.

BUT in the void between Hilda and the Trojans was neither night nor day. The sun, a little moon, glowed red in the Zenith. And through the weird gray twilight loomed another moon, almost as large, Jupiter, the angry planet whose realm Bill was invading. Thus Bill drove toward the Tojans — toward Hector, Achilles, Agamemnon, Patroclus, Priam and Nestor, on which last Jeribald had his hideout.

Islets in the void, but islets rushing through that void in a mazy dance, obedient to their dancemaster, Jupiter. The group was more than five astronomical units from Earth, and beyond was only a single asteroid, Hidalgo, the most distant of all. Beyond the Trojans no man had ever penetrated, because the great bullying dancemaster, Jupiter, barred the way, or beckoned to a flaming death.

Now Nestor came into view. And off her shores, ablaze with solar lights, Bill saw Jeribald's ship at anchor. But there were other lights ablaze in the immense castle that Jeribald had built for himself on Nestor, where he kept his nectarines, after raiding them on the Hilda group. Huge, gray, gaunt, it loomed up through the twilight, challenging Bill's daring.

Castle or ship? Bill had swerved aside the moment that the ship came into his optoscope. His own was so much smaller, there was a chance he hadn't been seen. He rounded the irregular mass of Nestor and anchored a bare three hundred miles from Jeribald's vessel, hidden from it and also from the castle by a ridge of rocks.

"Bill, what are you going to do?" Astra pleaded.

Bill braked his g.e. auxiliary, and felt

Shoving the girl from him, he seized the controls

the *Girl Unknown* quivering under the gravitational strain. On Nestor a man needed more than half-ton boots; he needed a Jonesite gauge to prevent being pulled up to the skies like a fish out of water. Bill handed one to Astra, explaining to her to keep it on her person, another to Vulcan. He reckoned that drag would hold them.

"Get your pistol, Vulcan. We're going to take that ship," he said.

Astra screamed, "He'll blast you to annihilation. And what will I do then? I love you, Bill."

"I'm putting you ashore," said Bill. "If I don't come back, go to the castle. I guess Jeribald will save your life. And don't lose that gauge I gave you, or it'll be your finish."

"But he's expecting you at the castle. He's planning to talk business there."

"That's why I'm going to the ship instead," said Bill.

Their pultex air-masks over their heads, the three went through the lock. But the bubbles in the eye-lenses showed that there was air on Nestor, and they threw back their hoods and went ashore. Astra cried, and clung to Bill, but he forced her roughly away. He had made his plans. Jeribald wouldn't dream he would dare attack the ship; once master of it, he could hold the castle under the threat of the neutron gun and exact what terms he chose.

But he meant to kill Jeribald, for Houghton and little Danny Briggs were crying in his heart for vengeance.

He looked at Vulcan. "Ready?" he asked.

"Qui'e rea'y, Mas'er," said Vulcan.

The Martian was a mechanical adept, like all his race. No need to explain the Jonesite gauge to him. Slowly Bill turned the handle from ten to eight, shutting off the interior power. Now he was rocking on his feet. Seven — and he soared upward through the air, pulling his hood about his head. Six — and his flight accelerated as the pull of Jupiter overcame the Jonesite counterpoise. Five — four, and Vulcan and he were flying arrow-like toward the ship, which was swiftly nearing.

Bill twirled the needle back to six and checked his flight. Vulcan, ahead of him, slowed too. Cautiously they drew near, approaching from the stern end, so as to be out of range of the swivel neutron gun.

LEW MERRILL was a pseudonym for the prolific Victor Rousseau Emanuel (1879-1960). He wrote for a staggering number of magazines, but "Lew Merrill" appeared primarily in Culture Publications' "Spicy" pulps — *Spicy-Stories*, *Spicy Mystery Stories*, etc. Later, the company became Trojan Publications, and the magazines changed names. The Merrill byline now appeared in *Speed Detective*, *Speed Western Stories*, *Super-Detective*, but the content was similar — two-fisted stories about hourglass-shaped women in danger. "Merril's" most famous work is "Bat-Man," a short-story in *Spicy Mystery Stories* (March, 1936) which has no connection to the famous DC Comics character.

Seven — and Bill moved forward no faster than a fish swims. He grasped the near fin of the propeller and swung himself through the lock.

Instantly he heard ribald shouts and laughter coming from the interior. He burst through the inner door, into the midst of Jeribald's ruffians. Tuck he recognized instantly by his belly-girth, but Garrou wasn't there. Instead, there were three others, whose faces seemed familiar; probably Bill had seen them on Hungaria, where Jeribald had signed them on. Each of the four held a girl upon his knee, a nectarine, of course, picked up by Jeribald from the outer planetoids. The girls were laughing. The air stank with the smell of liquor.

Before any of the startled men could pull a pistol, Bill had fired. His weapon blasted Tuck into a smouldering cinder. One of the others leaped, and a streak from Bill's pistol whipped his arm from his shoulder. The man dropped, screeching horribly. A whisp of ray drew a black line across Bill's check, and the pain rocked him. He fired, and the third man was down, the look of amazement ludicrous upon his blackening face. The flame of the fourth man's pistol shot over Bill's head. The two collided, staring at each other, and then Vulcan's shot drew a black hemisphere upon the other's cheek, and he fell, instantly dead, his withered tongue protruding from the blackened corner of his mouth.

BILL turned to the cowering girls. "Where's Ursula?" he shouted.

They didn't understand, but one, bolder than the rest, came sidling forward with arms outstretched and quivering haunches. Bill thrust her away, ran to the hold entrance and pulled off the hatch cover. He leaped down. It was almost dark within, but it was light enough for him to see that Ursula wasn't there. In the castle, then. Bill scampered up again. He heard a muffled outcry. Vulcan and Blacky, Jeribald's man at the controls, were in deadly combat. But no Martian would kill a Martian. Even an Earth-man wouldn't kill a Martian, which brought bad luck. The two were rolling over and over and pummeling each other.

But Jeribald's ship was now outside Jeribald's castle, and three neutron guns were covering her at a distance of a few yards with their slender muzzles. Blacky had worked the trick while Bill was fighting with Jeribald's crew.

Upon a platform just beneath the muzzles of the guns were Jeribald, Garrou, Ursula and Astra. Ursula's robe had been stripped from her, and for the first time Bill saw the rounded curves of her, the softness of her breasts. Even in that moment of despair a thrill went through him.

"Bill!" she cried, stretching out her arms to him.

Bill sprang to her and clasped her to him, feeling new strength fill him at the pressure of her soft body. Holding her, he looked up at Jeribald.

"You think you've won," he said.

"It looks like it — it looks like it, Sparling," sneered Jeribald through his black beard. He raised his voice. "Tuck!" he called.

Bill laughed. "Tuck's dead. So are the rest," he said. "I wish you'd been there, you damned murderer."

Garrou was covering him with his gun.

Astra, beside him, was mouthing viciously at Bill. "You poor fool, Jeribald left me orders to bring you to him," she scoffed.

"Very pretty," said Bill. "So — what?"

Jeribald took Bill's neutron pistol from his unresisting hand. "Well, you can guess, Sparling," he answered. "You've been a damned pest on the Jonesite grounds for a long time, and I'd already earmarked that claim you staked out. Get back into the ship!"

He waved Bill back. Ursula screamed and clung to him. Garrou forced her away. Bill went berserk then. He leaped at Garrou and struck him a blow that sent him reeling. Jeribald's obscene laugh drowned Ursula's cries.

"Don't be a fool, Sparling," he said. "Maybe I can use you after all. We'll talk later."

He shouted, and a dozen Martians came swarming out of the castle. They seized Bill and dragged him into the ship, and down into the hold.

But, as he was pulled past the controls, Bill saw Vulcan on the floor, fast asleep. This was his Martian sleeping-time, like that of all the Martian races, adjusted to the long night and day of their planet. Nothing could wake Vulcan till his sleep-period was over.

RAGING, Bill crouched in the hold, under the guard of the Martians. They had no neutron guns, but even one of the wiry little fellows was more than a match for the strongest Earth-man, apart from the paralyzing sting each carried in his stump of a tail.

He hadn't been there long before other Martians appeared, driving a bevy of nude nectarines before them — Jeribald's plunder of the inner asteroids. Young, half-afraid, yet laughing, and all excited by the prospect of the visit to Earth, they trooped in until the hold was filled with them. They had been anointed and perfumed in Jeribald's castle. That perfume, filling the stagnant air, was designed to allure. In the press of the jostling girls, Bill felt his head begin to swim, his mind to wander.

Ursula — Astra — what was one woman more or less? Life was rich among the planetoids, with wealth to be gained, and women for the asking. If Jeribald intended to make him an offer, was he going to refuse, and go to certain death?

On the other hand, Bill didn't feel that there was room in the same universe for Jeribald and himself. If only he had some weapon ...

He had slipped his Jonesite gauge into his shirt. It was of old-fashioned magnetic steel, hard enough to break a man's head with, but only eight inches long. A fantastic weapon ... Bill's brain began to clear. He pushed away the girls who jostled him. He must think only of Ursula.

Garrou came toward him, leering at the nectarines. In his right hand was a pistol. He motioned Bill to precede him, up the steps out of the hold, onto the stern deck.

Jeribald was there, with Ursula and Astra, a group of Martians about them. Astra snarled and spat at Bill as he approached. Jeri-bald said:

"I've been thinking about what I'll do with you. I don't throw things or men away when I can use them. This damned girl's been holding me off. I've made your life

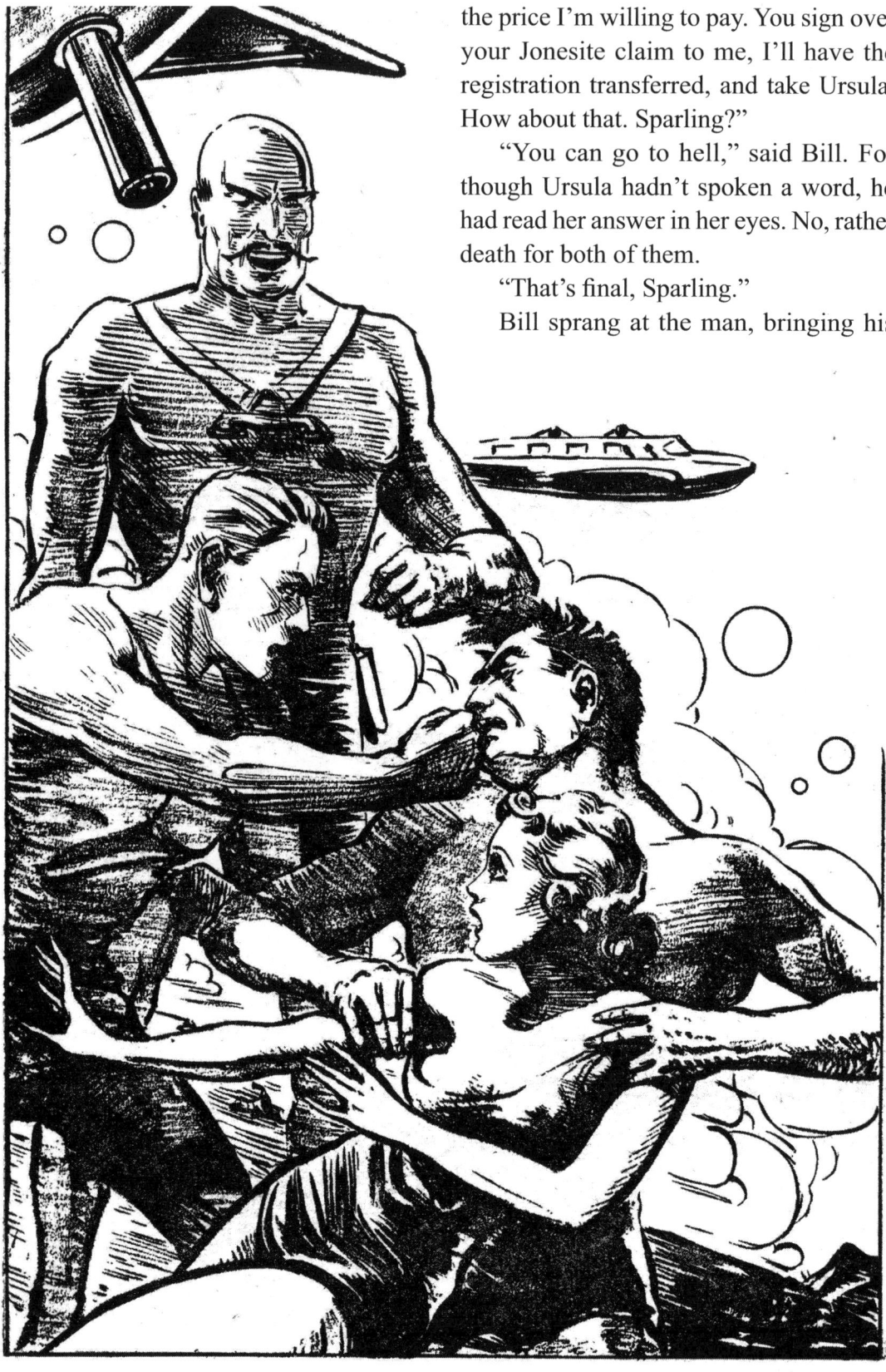

the price I'm willing to pay. You sign over your Jonesite claim to me, I'll have the registration transferred, and take Ursula. How about that. Sparling?"

"You can go to hell," said Bill. For though Ursula hadn't spoken a word, he had read her answer in her eyes. No, rather death for both of them.

"That's final, Sparling."

Bill sprang at the man, bringing his

gauge down in a sweeping stroke. He missed Jeribald's head, but the heavy implement slashed Jeribald's ear and half-severed it.

With a howl of rage and pain, Jeribald snatched Garrou's neutron pistol from his hand and leveled it — then checked himself.

"Bury them both!" he shrieked, dabbing at his ear. "I'll watch them die — die slow! Into the lock with them!"

Prepared for the worst though he was, Bill's blood ran cold with the realization of the fate in store for him. The slow descent, foot by foot, toward Jupiter, increasing — while Jeribald's ship kept pace, so that he could gloat over them. The quickening tempo of the flight, until Ursula and he would spin with inconceivable velocity, hour after hour, toward the giant planet, fully conscious, until its heat engulfed them.

In that moment everything about Bill was preternaturally clear. He saw the castle, and another bevy of nude girls on the platform in front of it; he saw the pain-distorted face of Jeribald, with Garrou at his side, and Astra, spitting out curses. His gaze went forward — and then he saw that it wasn't Blacky at the wheel, but Vulcan.

The Martian had somehow awakened, at the very beginning of his long sleep — out of loyalty to his master, as Bill thought afterward. And Blacky lay beside Vulcan, looking as if he had been stunned, his stumpy tail feebly twitching.

Ursula and Bill were seized and flung into the lock. The door closed on them.

"I'm ready to die, dearest," said the girl. "I know you came for me, didn't you? Poor dad! They murdered him while he was asleep. I'm glad we're dying together, Bill."

She moved toward him, and then his arms were about her, holding her fast, and her arms were around his neck. They'd go together into eternity in that way.

A lever clanged, the outer door of the lock opened; the two were hurled into the void. Suddenly Bill laughed. Why, Ursula had no pul-tex over her, no mask. She would freeze painlessly to death in a moment, even before she suffocated in the airless depths.

AND all the while Bill held the Jonesite gauge in his hand, and had forgotten.

Not far away he saw his own ship lying offshore. He saw Jeribald's ship suddenly careen upward, like a startled horse. Saw it all in the first instant of their plunge, felt himself and Ursula dragged slowly away from the shore of Nestor; then saw a chance of life for both of them — a hope — the surety.

He shot the indicator to the bottom of his gauge, turning on the full force of the emanations from the Jonesite within. Pull against pull — a little Jonesite gauge against the vast power of Jupiter. Instantly the movement ceased. And, lying oscillating in the atmosphere around the planet, Bill began striking a course toward his own ship.

But as he did so he saw Jeribald's ship shoot like a rocket toward Jupiter and disappear.

He swam through the air, dragging Ursula with him. She lay against his breast,

(Continued on page 132)

'Soldier' had become a dirty word, but Tony Blaine sought adventure. He learned the military's next step forward lay in the dormant past.

The Robbers

By E. C. TUBB

On his eighteenth birthday Tony Blain shocked his parents almost to hysteria by announcing his intention of doing something which was never mentioned in polite society.

"Join?" His mother, fifty but still beautiful, stared helplessly at his father, sixty but still upright and active. "The Service?" The way she said it made the word sound unclean.

"That's right." Tony stared defiantly down at the soft carpet.

"Nonsense!" His father came over to him and dropped a hand on his shoulder. "You can't mean it, Tony, not a well-brought up boy like you. I'm surprised at your even mentioning it before your mother, it's ... It's indecent."

"What's indecent about it?" Tony tried not to hear his mother's muffled sobs. "All I want to do is to join the Service."

"Now you're being silly." His father bit his lips as he remembered the books on child psychology. "Why don't we talk this over man to man? You don't want to upset your mother, do you? And I know that you wouldn't like to upset me." He laughed, a forced, unnatural sound, but his eyes behind their contact lenses held a hint of worry. "If that Johnny Parker's been filling your head ... "

"Johnny had nothing to do with it." Tony squirmed from beneath the parental hand, wishing that his father would realise that he had grown up and was no longer a child. "I just want to join the service."

"But why?" His mother dabbed at her eyes with a scrap of lace. "Aren't you happy here?"

From her tone Tony knew that 'here' meant the house, their friends, his father's business, the world and, in short, the entire universe. He sighed as he tried to find the words which would convince them he was serious.

"Please." He fought the desire to cross the room and comfort his mother with promises to forget the whole business. "It isn't that I'm unhappy or miserable, it's just that I want to get away, see things for myself instead of on the video, *do* something for a change instead of following the same old round. I … "

He paused as he saw their blank expressions, knowing that his words were literally meaningless to them. "I just want to join the Service."

"I've never heard of anything so disgusting in my whole life!" His father paced the floor in his anger. " Here you are, a decently brought up boy — a boy with everything to look forward to and without a worry in the entire world — wanting to run off and join that gang of criminal scum. I won't allow it, do you hear? I won't allow it!"

"You can't stop me," reminded Tony quietly. "I'm of age."

"You're only a baby," wailed his mother. "You're too young to know what's best. Listen to your father before you do anything you may be ashamed of later. The Service!" She shuddered as if he had said an unforgivable obscenity.

"But … "

"Your mother's right, Tony," snapped his father. "It's about time the Service was closed down good and for all. It's nothing but a source of trouble and a menace to decent people. We had the same trouble with the Colonisation Project years ago, though at least they did offer something concrete, and I can tell you that if they hadn't stopped recruiting they would have been shut down. This Service business is getting a little too much for decent people to stomach and I forbid you to even think about it again."

"Yes, sir."

"After all what do we need it for?" His father was like a dog with a big juicy bone and he couldn't stop worrying it. "*We* don't need soldiers. *We* don't have wars. *We* live in peace. As I was telling the others at the club the whole idea of the Service is to find jobs for incompetents who would starve if ever they had to pit their brains against real business men." His smirk left no doubt that he classified himself as a 'real' business man. "If it wasn't for the way they taint the minds of our youth the whole business would be a farce and I'm really surprised that any boy would even consider giving up home and comfort, the love of his parents, and a safe snug future to join up with those uniformed fools."

"Yes, sir." Tony hoped that his voice held the right amount of dutiful obedience.

"I'm glad that you see it my way, son. When you remember all that we've done for you, you'll realise that it's only your simple duty to forget this nonsense. You know the plans I have for you, the things your mother and I have decided. There's a place in the office just waiting for a bright young man to step into and within a few years, twenty or thirty say, I wouldn't be surprised to see you sitting in my chair." His father grinned with self-conscious embarrassment. "I'll be getting a little old by then, of course, but I'll still be able to bounce my grandson on my knee."

Tony sighed, feeling the imponderable weight of inertia forcing him back into his predetermined destiny. The plan was simple. First college, then the office and routine work for thirty years or until his father decided to retire, and with the modern life expectancy what it was, a man remained active and alert for over a century. There would be a child, a pre-determined son or, if he were very lucky, a girl and a boy both. All planned, all taken care of, all decided by his too-loving, too-possessive parents and a benevolent, patriarchal government.

The thought of it made him writhe.

***

The recruiting officer was a big, scar-faced man with eyes like chips of granite and a sneering, contemptuous mouth. He leaned back in his chair, not speaking, staring at the youngster, waiting for him to break the silence. It was an elementary trick in psychology. Too elementary. Tony didn't speak.

"Well?" the officer finally snapped. "What do you want?"

"I want to join up."

"Join up, what? Tie-rails? Curtains?"

"I want to join the Service," said Tony quietly. The man's reactions disappointed him. He had expected to be greeted with open arms and pleased interest but so far he had only met cold indifference and blank hostility.

"So you want to join the Service." The officer nodded as if at a child. "Why?"

"Why?" Tony blinked. His real reason was that he was bored with the safe monotony of life at home and wanted a change. The only other way he could leave Earth without spending a lot of money he didn't have was to join the Service and he had imagined they would have welcomed any new recruit with open arms. Apparently he had been wrong.

"Don't you want recruits?"

"Perhaps." The officer shrugged as he opened a drawer and pulled out a printed form. "You haven't answered my question."

"Must I? I would have thought that the mere fact I'm offering to join would have been its own answer."

"You think so?" The officer stared up from beneath his lowered brows. "Look, friend, if you knew how many snotty-nosed kids I get in here you'd think differently. Every time one of them has a row at home they come crying to join up and every one of them backs out after the first couple of days. Now? Why do you want to join?"

"I want to do something with my life," said Tony slowly. "I feel stifled at home and want to get out and away from it all."

"So you've decided that the Service can provide an escape route?" There was no mistaking the sneer in the man's voice. Tony flushed.

"Perhaps, but what is it to you what my reasons are? You want men don't you?"

"We want the right kind of men," corrected the officer. He stared at the young man. "Look. You've asked to join us — we didn't ask to join you. Now, for the last time, just why do you want to join?"

"I want to escape the rat-trap I'm in," snapped Tony. "I want to plan my own life instead of having it all done for me. I want a chance to travel and see things as they are instead of over the video. I want … "

"You want to fight?"

"Fight?" Tony swallowed at the interruption and struggled to accept a new concept. "Kill, you mean?"

"Men don't fight for fun," said the officer drily. "You know what the Service is, don't you? You know that we keep order out among the new worlds. That means that you'll have to fight. Well?"

"I'll fight," said Tony without hesitation. "Can I join?"

"That's better." The officer made several notations on the form. Name? Age? Residence? Educational qualifications? Any disease? Tony answered mechanically as the officer filled out the form. "Parental consent?"

"No."

"No?"

"I don't need it," said Tony defiantly. "I'm of age."

"I see." More scratch marks and a scrawling signature. "Sign here and press the ball of your right thumb there." The man watched as Tony completed the form. "Right. You're now a provisional member of the Service. There will be a week of examinations and inoculations and during that time you will be able to exercise your right of quittance. After that time you are bound body and soul for the next ten years. Better decide one way or the other as soon as you can — ten years can be a long time where you're going."

"I'll stay."

"I hope so." The officer pointed towards a door. "Go through there, an orderly will attend you and you must do everything you're told." He held out his hand. "Good luck, soldier."

Tony smiled as he took the proffered hand. *Soldier!* The word had a nasty flavour but he supposed that he would get used to it, just as he would get used to the harsh paint instead of the soft pastels at home, the obsolete devices and the unperfumed air. In any case he still had a week to decide.

The officer watched the young man disappear through the doorway then thumbed the button of an intercom on his desk.

"Yes?"

"Benson here. A new one coming through."

"Good?"

"Perhaps. I think that we'll be able to use him."

"Report?"

"The usual thing. Frustration at parental control, wanderlust, revolt against stultifying security, romantic imagination and the usual self-interest." He chuckled. "Aggressive too."

"Good. We'll give him the works and see how he reacts." The unseen speaker sighed. "I wish that we could get more."

"So do I," said Benson feelingly. He opened the circuit and sat grimly behind his desk.

Waiting.

***

The training was queer. Like all his generation, Tony knew nothing of war or military strategy and had always been told that war and soldiers were complementary and unpleasant. Earth had been free of internecine conflict for more than five hundred years and even the historical videos and educational tapes only mentioned war as something best forgotten. So much had the desire for peace become ingrained in the race that the Service, the sole surviving branch of the armed forces, was considered as something not nice to talk about, much as the prisons of an earlier age in their own time.

But even so the training seemed queer.

In fact it was more than queer, it verged on the insane. The business of marching in strict tempo, of slamming delicate feet hard against unyielding concrete, of making ridiculous gestures whenever meeting an officer and of forcing the body into mechanical posturing. Then there was the stupid, niggling, almost insulting insistence on non-essentials. The polishing of metal which basically could not take a high polish. The staining of equipment with temporary stain when it was obvious that a plasta-film would have served the same purpose with less effort and, most infuriating of all, the demand that everything be kept exactly in its place without deviation and without reason.

Tony stuck it out for five weeks, waiting all the time for some sign that would convince him it was all in fun or had some deeper more basic reason than any he had been able to find, and then, when none was forthcoming, protested.

The reaction made him mentally ill.

It wasn't the physical side so much as the sheer stupidity of what they made him do. Routine work, useless, done to shouted commands and hostile eyes. He dug a trench — and then filled it in again. He scrubbed a floor, using a brush not more than two inches square — and then had to dirty it in order to scrub it again. The explosion came when they told him to sweep the parade ground with a hand broom when a standard though archaic broom stood against a wall.

"You refuse?" The loud-voiced sweaty faced man who seemed to take a sensual delight in inventing newer and more stupid tasks glared at the young man.

"Yes." Tony deliberately refused to stiffen to attention. "I refuse to have my intelligence insulted by such tasks."

"You know what this means of course? You are under military discipline now and you can be shot for refusing to obey an order."

"Go ahead and shoot," said Tony wearily. "If the Service is composed of men like you and jobs like this I'll be insane before the ten years are up anyway. Kill me if you want to, but let's not have any more of this stupidity."

"You … " The man swallowed then, incredibly, smiled with what he obviously imagined to be a warm friendliness. "Now don't be a fool, son. Discipline is essential in any army and these things have got to be put up with."

"Why?"

"You shouldn't ask that. Orders is orders and that's all there is to it. Now get on with it, lad, and I'll forget what you said."

"No."

"Don't be a fool! You're in the Service now and you've got to do as you're told. What would happen if everyone did as they liked? You've got to learn to obey."

"Why?"

"It doesn't matter why. You're a ranker and rankers aren't supposed to think, only to obey. Now. Sweep that parade ground."

"All right — but only if I can use the big broom."

THE ROBBERS — Originally published in *New Worlds*, December 1954.
Copyright © 1954 by E.C. Tubb.
Reprinted by permission of Cosmos Literary Agency for the author's estate.
(Cover by Gerard A. Quinn)

"You'll use the hand broom."

"Why?" Tony kept his voice even, genuinely interested in the answer. "If you want the ground swept isn't it logical to use the best method available? I could do the job five times faster with the big broom."

"You'll use the broom you're given or you'll be in trouble, serious trouble." The sweaty-faced man thinned his lips as if savouring an expected pleasure. "We've had men of your sort here before, cocky, self-confident kids who think they know it all. Believe me, son, they soon change their minds. We've a place here, a nice, secluded place where they learn sense and discipline." He sucked at his lips. "Now, for the last time, get sweeping or I'll report you for insubordination."

"You mean that you'd use physical force against me?"

The concept was one Tony found hard to believe. Physical aggression had gone out with organized war and he found it almost impossible to realize that, unless he agreed to sublimate his intelligence, they would torture him. That would be too barbaric and against all the accepted codes of moral conduct.

"I'm not saying anything except that unless you do as you're told, when you're told, without any argument or question, you'll suffer for it." The sweaty man pointed towards the small broom and the vast expanse of ground. "Sweep."

For a moment Tony hesitated then, as the utter absurdity of the command returned with fresh impact, he shook his head.

"No."

"So you still refuse." The sweaty man shrugged and blew sharply on a whistle around his neck. "You'll be sorry, son. Believe me, you'll be sorry."

They took Tony to the secluded place reserved for those who didn't obey without question. They kept him there for twelve weeks and when they released him he seemed to have aged ten years. He also had an intense hatred for all things military.

***

Commander Gerard eased his bulk in the too-small chair and glanced impatiently at the psychologist. "Well?"

French sighed as he put down the thin sheaf of papers. "As expected. Forty percent of those volunteering have revolted against conditions which they assume insult their intelligence. Fifty percent have accepted the conditions and the remaining ten percent broke beneath the strain and were returned to civilian life there to spread the ghastly horror and criminal tendencies of the Service." The way he said it didn't make it a joke.

"The percentage of those revolting is creeping up," reminded Gerard. "We don't have to worry about those who broke."

"We may have to. Already there is too much popular feeling against the Service and there has been agitation for the government to shut us down. If we return many more to spread the tales of hate and distortion then we may have a real problem on our hands."

"We won't be shut down," said the Commander with quiet conviction. He riffled the thin sheaf of papers. "My worry is that there aren't enough volunteers. We're getting the females all right, they have little to look forward to now that the genetics bureau has enforced birth control so rigidly, but the males are slow in coming forward and those we do get aren't all of the right type." He looked hopefully at the psychologist. "Maybe if we lowered the standards?"

"No." French sounded very definite. "Don't let yourself be thrown off by quantity instead of quality. We've tried the other way and it didn't work, as things are it couldn't work, and it wouldn't work if we tried it again. You know that, Gerard. Don't let's waste time going over old ground."

"You're right, I suppose," admitted the commander and stared sombrely at the papers lying on his desk. "But we're getting so few now, less than we've ever had before. What the hell's wrong with the youth of today?"

"Age."

"What?"

"Old age." French shrugged at the commander's expression. "The Earth is being stifled by the dead hand of too many old men in too many high places. With the life expectancy what it is a man lives too long, has too much power, and, because he is old, is grimly determined to hang on to that power for as long as he can. We have no wars now, no famine, no disease and the death rate has fallen to a miraculous low. But the Earth can only support a certain number of people, Gerard, and unless the old die there can be no room for the young. So we get stringent birth control and the rationing of children to bare replacements of those who die."

"That makes sense."

"It makes good sense, but inevitably it leads to an unbalanced ecology. Parents are having their child or children very late in life. They are middle-aged when the infant is born and old when it reaches maturity. Old people are set in their ways and there can be no real contact between a father of sixty and a son of sixteen. There isn't just one generation between them, there is two, or there would have been in normal circumstances. The boy is isolated in a world of his own, surrounded by old men and women who, though they mean well, just can't sympathise with youthful hopes and dreams. To the aged security is everything and, when they have offered their children security, they imagine they have done the full sum of their duty. The rest, the mutual understanding, the sharing of ambition, the zest and enthusiasm, all that means nothing to them. They are too old to remember their own youth."

"But Earth is peaceful now and has been for five hundred years. Are you saying that a war would be a good thing?"

"For the race, no. For the individual, yes." French shrugged at the shocked, almost horrified expression on the commander's face. "I know how you feel about war, how every intelligent man must feel, but we are talking of a remedy for a specific disease. Racially speaking war is a disease and no race can ever hope for a balanced mental existence until it can get rid of it. War brings a tremendous emotional reaction, the victors have a guilt complex and, after victory, can only do one of two things. They can try to blot out the object of their guilt, eliminate its physical existence in an effort to eliminate their own shame, or they can try to make amends and, by gifts and help, seek to restore their one-time enemy to equal footing again. The first method was tried at Carthage by Rome when even the fields were sown with salt so that nothing should ever grow there again. The second method was tried twice running in Europe by England with Germany. Neither method was successful."

"And yet you advocate war?"

"No. I advocate combat. You see, Gerard, man is an animal and must be treated as such. A man is basically savage, he sees a thing, he wants it; he fights to get it. Fighting, of course, like combat, need not mean physical struggle. It can be his wits against the wits of others, his desires against a system, his longing to do something against obstacles, either artificial or natural, which attempt to stop him. A youth must have this combat if he is to grow up mentally stable and, in the old days, war provided the thrill and excitement, the chance to break away from the rut and go adventuring."

"I begin to see what you mean," said Gerard slowly. "War is bad, no one can honestly make out a case for war and no intelligent man would try. Perhaps that is why the old civilisations collapsed and, in a way, it was a good thing they did."

"Yes, but we are still left with the need for providing combat for our youth. We haven't got that combat on Earth. A boy grows up and every step of his youth is planned by old men and women. He wants a thing and, because the old dote on their children, he gets it for the asking. He is protected from trouble, shielded from want, and, every time he tries to strike out on his own he is stopped by well-worn clichés. 'Your father knows best, son,' or 'Old heads are wise heads,' or 'You'll know better when you grow up.' No answers, no combat, nothing you can get your teeth into. I tell you, Gerard the youth of today is smothering in a mental bog of over-affection and a parental inability to identify age with youth. It is almost as if there are two races instead of one.

"And there is another thing. A race must grow, expand; spread out with new enterprises and new ventures. Age doesn't do that. The old want things to remain as they are, as they always have been. Age is static and any race which becomes static is on the road to cultural death." French picked up the thin sheaf of papers again and flipped them in his hands. "That is why these people are so important. Without them the human race is in grave danger of dying from age-induced sterility and mental ossification." He glanced at the commander. "That is why we can have no mercy, no regrets; no second thoughts about what we do. That is the reason why we are here and, personally, I think it a good reason."

Gerard nodded.

***

Tony crouched, naked but for a loin cloth, and flexed his hands as they swung at his sides. Above him the sun shone hot and bright from a childless sky and the soft turf of the field made a rolling carpet of green beneath his feet. He was fit, tanned, and muscles rippled beneath his skin where no muscles had ever shown before. He still couldn't understand the reason for the peculiar training they had given him ever since he had been released from the prison, but now it was more bearable and at least they did answer his questions.

"The reason you are being taught to fashion a sharp cutting edge from a selected piece of stone is that there may be occasions when you will need to know how it is done. Metal tools wear, are lost, rust to dullness and are hard to replace. Now — taking the flint in the left hand you support it against the left thigh and bear down with the … "

And on another occasion:

"The principal of the bow and arrow is fundamentally simple and is being taught to you in order that, should you ever require missile weapon, you will know how to make one. The bow should be a strong piece of springy material, wood, bone, even metal will answer. The thong can be made from a strip of hide, sinew, woven threads … "

And again:

"It is important that you should know how to produce fire at will for the purposes of signalling, heat and light. Sparks may be struck from stones of a selected nature, a flint and … "

Some of it made sense. It was logical that he might be cast away on some planet, crash for example, and such knowledge would help him to survive until help came. But other items puzzled him. The training in building stone houses and dwellings from dirt and woven reeds. The teaching which seemed to concern itself with the sanitary arrangements should he ever find himself in a native village. The long, headache-producing sessions of hypnotic teaching and the continuous repetition of certain aspects of training until he knew them backwards and more, until his body moved in automatic reflex action.

And now this.

He squinted at the far side of the meadow and began to move cautiously forward. There was an animal somewhere in the field, a dangerous animal, and he was supposed to find it and fetch it back to the compound. How he was supposed to do it he didn't know.

The sun was very warm, the air heavy and sweet with the odours of growing things, and, as he moved forward over the rolling turf, his mind kept returning to the inevitable problem. At first he had been eager then, when he had realised the illogical stupidity of what he had to do, he had protested. Punishment had followed, degrading, almost insane punishment and now he had nothing but hatred and contempt for that part of the Service. But, strangely enough, he had enjoyed these past few months with their relative freeness from irksome restrictions and the flow of interesting, if basically useless knowledge.

It was fun to make a flint knife, but that's all it was or ever could be. Knowledge like that had no commercial value and the likelihood of ever needing a sharp edge made from native stone was so remote as to be almost inconceivable. The same with the bow and arrow, the methods of making fire, the tricks he had learned as to how to knot a cord and dig a furrow. Useless knowledge, wasteful pursuits and ridiculous, illogical concentration of effort. Why learn how to use a bow when even the crudest rifle would have been so much better? It would have been interesting to learn how to make ammunition or the propelling charges, and a knowledge of explosives would have surely been of more use than knowing how to build a hut.

He began to wonder about the entire scheme of training and, as he thought about it, his contempt for the Service mounted. Stupid actions without sense or logic and now stupid knowledge without use or purpose. The Service was rumoured to be a fighting corps, battling across the galaxy with speeding ships and iron men. They had a long heritage and enforced law and order among the scattered stars with grim determination. That was how some people thought of them. Others, his father among them, had considered the Service to be a resting place for morons, incompetents, useless wasters who couldn't do a decent day's work to save their lives. An unnecessary growth on the new society which should be amputated and left to dissolve in its own slime.

Which was right? Tony didn't know, though, as he walked carelessly over the grass, he tended to believe that his father held the correct opinion.

The animal saw him first!

A low growl coincided with a rush of displaced air and a heavy body, wide-jawed and white-fanged, leapt from the grass and drove towards his throat.

Instinct saved him, the automatic response of his trained body to the unexpected. He dropped, feeling the skin of his back burn to the touch of raking claws, then he had spun away from the spot, his heart pounding against his ribs as he looked at the animal he was supposed to capture and take back to the compound.

It was a mutated hybrid half-dog, half-wolf, a low-bodied, red-eyed, gape-mouthed creature with a shaggy coat and a lashing tail. It snarled as Tony stared at it, writhing its lips back from gleaming fangs then, wriggling on its belly, it tensed for the spring.

Fear rooted Tony where he stood for almost too long. He stared at the animal as if at a scene on a video programme and it was only when the shaggy body had launched itself at his throat that he jerked aside. Even so the impact of the animal's body threw him to the ground and immediately he was fighting desperately for his life.

At first he couldn't believe it. Physical combat was something utterly strange to his concepts of normal living and he struggled more to prevent the animal ripping out his throat than to inflict injury in turn. Blood gushed from a torn place on his shoulder, sharp claws raked his naked thighs and saliva spotted his face. Frantically he rolled on the soft grass, half-sick from the creature's foul breath, and whimpered as he felt fangs meet in the loose skin of his arm.

He kicked, managed somehow to get to his feet, and ran desperately towards the edge of the field and the safety of the compound. After him bounded the hybrid.

Tony grunted as the weight of the lunging beast landed on his back, tripping and falling as he clawed at the shaggy coat. Now, for the first time, anger began to replace his sick fear. Rage sent adrenalin to accelerate his heart and hate replaced the cold dread of what might be. Though he didn't know it his lips writhed back from his teeth in emulation of those of the animal, and suddenly, without thought or reason, he reverted back to what his race had once been.

He snarled, his brows knitting over his eyes, his chin tight against his chest to protect his throat from the hungry fangs, and his hands sank deep into the fur around the whip-cord throat of the snarling beast. Grimly he held on, fighting the frenzied clawing of the animal, ignoring the hammer-blows from its back feet, his thumbs digging deeper and deeper into the yielding windpipe. Blood spattered him and his skin gaped with a dozen wounds, but still he held on. Now he knew that he had to kill or be killed. Now he knew that there was no mercy, no understanding, nothing between him and extinction but the strength in his body and the will to survive.

And he intended to survive.

It seemed to take an incredibly long time. It seemed that the virile life of the creature would never die, that he had gripped the lashing throat for an eternity. Then, slowly at first, the struggling faded, the snarling turned into a whimper, the whimper into a strangled wine and, with a final convulsion, the animal jerked, twisted, and collapsed in a silent heap.

Numbly Tony climbed to his feet and, staggering a little, swung the heavy body to his shoulders and walked towards the distant compound. His wounds burned and the sight of his own blood made him feel ill, but worse than that was the knowledge that he had fought like an animal and killed like a beast.

He paused to vomit, his face shining with sweat as he relived the struggle, his flesh cringing away from the hairy touch of the dead beast. Again, in imagination he saw the gaping jaws, the red eyes, smelt the foul odour and felt the wet touch of dripping saliva. He had won the battle but he took no pride in the winning. He had killed but was ashamed of having brought death to a living creature.

And he had acted like a fool.

They had warned him that the beast was dangerous. He should have found a stone, a pair of stones, one for throwing and the other to use as a club. He had been incredibly lucky and he sweated again as he thought of all the things that could have happened to him. His fingers severed by those razor fangs, his wrist gripped and broken, his face slashed, his eyes …

He swallowed against rising nausea and was hardly conscious of reaching the compound. A man took the dead thing from his shoulders, whistled as he saw his wounds, and steadied him as he stumbled and almost fell.

"Take it easy, boy, it's all over now."

"All over?" Tony shook his head, not understanding what the other meant. "It would have killed me," he muttered. "You would have let it kill me."

"That's right."

"You admit it?" Shock and horror brought back the sick nausea. "But why? Why?"

Blackness surged around him before he could hear the answer.

***

It was very quiet in the office, not even the muted hum of an air conditioner broke the silence and Tony fidgeted as he stared at the two men seated opposite him at the desk. He was here because he had asked to be here, because he had determined to find out what it was all about and had demanded and insisted until they had granted an interview.

Commander Gerard cleared his throat and put down the report he had been reading.

"You're a little late, Blain," he said mildly. "I expected you at least a week ago."

"I was in hospital then, recovering from the wounds that animal gave me." Tony tried hard not to reveal his surprise at what the older man had said. Expect him?

"Of course, I had forgotten." The commander smiled as he stared at the young man. "And now you want to know what all this is about."

"Yes."

"Naturally." Gerard looked at the young man and sighed. These interviews were nothing new to him, he welcomed them, but each time they differed in trifles and differed most in number. Once he had interviewed them in batches of a score or more, then in tens, then fives, now it was down to singles. He wondered when the stream would finally cease. "Would you mind telling us," he said carefully, "just what you think the Service is?"

"I don't know just what it is," said Tony evenly. "But I know what it *isn't*. For one thing it isn't a military force and I doubt if it could ever fight a war."

"Oh? Why do you say that?"

"For one thing your system of training is directly opposite to the results expected from any fighting man. A soldier should be able to use his initiative, take short cuts and reduce his work to an optimum level. He … "

"You're quite wrong, you know," said Gerard evenly, and remembered not to smile. "The Service could fight a war. Fight it in the only way any war should be fought — in utter extermination of both warring sides. The training you mention was basic for many years during the Period of Combat, and those old-time warriors were expert in producing the kind of material they needed. The only thing which has altered is that you are of a much higher intelligence than they were. Too intelligent in fact to make any kind of a soldier, much less a good one."

He smiled at Tony's expression and

turned to the psychologist. "Perhaps you would care to enlighten our young friend?"

"Discipline is based on the utter sublimation of both the intellect and the imagination," said French curtly. "An intelligent man usually has a vivid imagination and that means he can visualise the results of many actions. A good soldier, good from an officer viewpoint, is a man who does not think but merely obeys. That principal still holds true. We must have men who will do as they are told *when* they are told without question or hesitation. Hesitation could mean the loss of a strategical advantage and question makes the whole concept of war ridiculous. Once a soldier starts to question why, then he is both useless and dangerous to his own command. I trust that you can understand why this is?"

Tony nodded realising only too well from his own reactions just what would happen in a closely integrated force if the personnel should start to question every order as to its logic or validity. Men would no longer perform acts of blind heroism — their logic and imagination would combine to prevent them acting before they had considered the worth of what they did, and, once they visualised the risks and dangers, they would hesitate and be reluctant instead of swift and daring. But that still didn't answer his question.

"I know what you're thinking," said Gerard. "But remember this. The Service is the only armed force in the known part of the galaxy and, as such, must have soldiers to operate. With the powers we have and the potential destruction within every ship, we must have men without imagination to service them. We want no idealists, no thinkers, no men who, during the long and wearying periods of flight, begin to dream up their own concepts of military empires. That means we want men without imagination and we find them during the initial period of training."

"I see." Tony stared thoughtfully at the fading scars on his arms. "Then what about … "

"You?" Gerard nodded. "You fall into a special category. That is why your training has been different since you displayed your determination not to fit into the soldier-pattern." He paused, staring at the intent face of the young man. "You," he said deliberately, "are a colonist."

"A colonist!" For a moment Tony stared at the commander wondering whether or not the man was serious, then he shook his head.

"You are surprised?"

"Yes."

"Why?"

"Because either you're joking with me or you don't know what you're talking about. You say that I'm to be a colonist and I suppose you mean that I've been selected to help found a new settlement on one of the habitable planets, but it just doesn't make sense. What training have I been given? I haven't learned anything of technology, of science, of how to maintain and operate equipment. What good would I be in any settlement?"

"What do you think a colony is, Blain?" French leaned forward as he rapped the question.

"A settlement of men and women who start a new centre of civilisation." Tony droned the words mechanically, without any real thought.

"Exactly. And what equipment do you think they need to do that?"

"I don't know. A pile perhaps for power, domes to live in. food plants and machine tools. Some mining machinery, farming equipment, transport vehicles and radio communication. Factories and assembly belts, doctors and scientists to study the ecology," he shrugged. "A lot of *things*."

"Too many *things*. Far too many for the ships we have and the worlds that are waiting." The psychologist leaned back in his chair. "We tried that way once, you may remember the Colonisation Project, and it failed. People who went to the stars wanted to take Earth with them. They wanted everything they had become accustomed to, their radios, their comforts, their easy living and protection against all danger. It couldn't be done and it never will be done. You can't shift the cultural pattern of a world and you can't transplant an entire civilisation. We tried to give them all the things you mentioned, but it wasn't enough. Mines had to be dug, water sources diverted, animals exterminated, the entire ecology of a planet changed to a simulacrum of Earth. We could do it with one world. We could do it given unlimited material, unlimited men, and a couple of centuries of time. But we haven't got that much time, Blain, and we know better than to repeat past errors.

"So we found another way. Space is vast, Blain, and there are hundreds of Earth-type worlds waiting to be colonised. There are too many for us to do more than map them, test their atmospheres for oxygen content, their water for purity. Men can live on those worlds — we think, but it would take twenty years and the full-time efforts of an entire group of scientists to turn a possibility into a certainty. We had to find a short cut, and *you* are it."

"The training," said Tony quietly. "How to make a knife from stone, a bow and arrow, and how to make fire. Simple things primitive things, the sort of things a man needs to know if ... "

"If he is alone, without the benefits of civilisation, dependant on himself and the knowledge we can give him." French nodded. "So now you know the whole purpose of the Service. It has a bad reputation — deliberately. We want only those volunteers who have the initial drive to leave their comforts and seek something adventurous and new. We sort them out, for we can always use the soldier-type, there are too many routine jobs to be done as it is. The rest, those who are strong enough to stay, become the colonists. We teach them all the things that men have forgotten during

(Continued on page 133)

NEXT ISSUE:
"Face to Infinity" by E.C. Tubb
**Learn more about the author in "Remembering E.C. ("Ted") Tubb"
by Philip Harbottle on the following page.**

Remembering E.C. ("Ted") Tubb

BY PHILIP HARBOTTLE

How do you introduce a publishing legend who has published hundreds of novels and short stories in more than ten languages across seven decades?

The Bold Venture Press editors invited me to pen a short article to introduce E.C. Tubb to the readers of *Pulp Adventures*. But where to begin?

E. C. Tubb's 1954 novel *The Resurrected Man* (forthcoming from Bold Venture) was only the third sf book I had ever read, following two pseudonymous titles by John Russell Fearn. Their impact on my 14-year old self was electrifying. Taking a newspaper round to earn extra pocket money, I spent every penny hunting out any science fiction books I could find by these authors.

Then in March 1964 I learned that Tubb would be attending the BSFA Easter convention, in Birmingham. A chance to meet my idol—but what could a shy neo-fan possibly say to him? Then I had an inspiration.

Clandestinely using my employer's office facilities after hours—risking being sacked if caught—I quickly wrote a 10,000-word illustrated thesis on Tubb's novels,

then stencilled and printed it.

At the convention hotel Tubb was surrounded by fans, but I finally managed to speak to him in his room. He was holding court alongside a young Mike Moorcock,

A legendary author of science fiction helped a fan go from amateur to professional.

Cover: Robert Gibson Jones

newly appointed as editor of *New Worlds*. I handed him a copy of *E. C. Tubb—An Evaluation* in a brown envelope, but my mumbled explanation was lost in the hubbub. He took it with a smile, set it aside, and invited me to have a drink with the rest of the crowd.

Days later I received a letter, signed "As ever, Ted," graciously thanking me for the surprise. He had thought my packet was "just another fanzine" at the time, and had not looked at it until he was on the train back to London. He was amazed that I had identified all his pseudonyms unaided.

He promised to keep me regularly informed of his future output, and we became friends and regular correspondents. Eventually, he would invite me to become his agent, and my tribute pamphlet

The self-published ice-breaker ...

"Evane" by E. C. Tubb

E. C. Tubb

would be used as the basis for my full-length book on Tubb's life and work, *The Tall Adventurer* (1999).

When I became editor of *Vision of Tomorrow* in 1969, Ted booked himself into a hotel for the weekend, and wrote three marvellous stories for my magazine. One of them, "Lucifer!" became recognized as a classic, winning the Europa Prize after being anthologized around the world. It is currently in development as a movie by Curmudgeon Films.

Edwin Charles Tubb was born in London in 1919. As a youth, he was an avid reader of the imported American SF pulp magazines, but the Second World War thwarted his nascent writing ambitions. Post-war he was in the vanguard of an emerging group of young British writers who included Arthur C. Clarke, John Wyndham, John Brunner, John Christopher and others, who laid the foundations for British sf development, working largely through the editorial direction of John Carnell. Tubb's first professional sale was to Carnell's *New Worlds*, and his first novel appeared a year later, in 1951.

Within a very short space of time, he was established as a novelist, and recognised as one of the leading contributors to sf magazines on both sides of the Atlantic.

His early sf novels were fast-moving action-adventure stories, a type of fiction demanded by the publishers. These novels are now valuable collectors' items, and have been reprinted world-wide. But for the more selective magazines, Tubb wrote a more thoughtful, psychological type of story, many of them genuine classics. He has been widely anthologized, most notably in several "World's Best" selections by Judith Merril, and Don Wollheim. In fact, there are well over 200 magazines stories, many of them of novelette length, under his own name and no less than 27 pseudonyms. But despite his many anthologizations and personal collections, the modern reader will search in vain for many of his stories, unless he has access to the increasingly rare original magazines.

Accordingly, your editors have selected one of Tubb's earliest unreprinted stories, "The Robbers" from a 1955 *New Worlds*. These early stories remain as fresh and exciting as the day they were published, displaying an astonishing range of themes and styles.

Over seven decades, Tubb published hundreds of sf stories and novels, as well as thrillers, western, supernatural, and historical fiction, gaining a dual reputation for colourful adventure stories, as well as challenging and thought-provoking pieces. He is perhaps best known for his long running "Dumarest of Terra" series of novels, and his *Space 1999* novelizations, all of which remain in print

Ted became my friend and mentor, eventually asking me to become his agent, and we rejoiced together as scores of his books were reprinted. I was thrilled to work with him on new books, including a truly wonderful final Dumarest, which he wrote for me—and his fans—despite failing health. He lived to see it published and acclaimed by Dumarest's many fans. But tragically, he died without knowing that a major UK publisher. Orion Books, was set to give digital E-Books immortality to his entire SF novel backlist of well over a hundred novels—and to book and E-publish his very last wonderful novel *Fires of Satan*, completed only a couple of weeks before he died.

I've loved the man and his work for over 50 years, and miss him terribly. But now I take pleasure in working for his grand daughter Lisa John, (his literary heir) to make sure that his work will continue to be reprinted and translated around the world. ■

Philip Harbottle manages Cosmos Literary Agency, representing the author's estate of E.C. Tubb and several other notable authors of science fiction, mystery and horror.

Sniffing Out the Rain Shadow

by Robert W. Walker

"DAMN it, dog, don't fall in," Luke Holley said in a calm, near whisper to Scout, his cadaver dog. There was no need to shout, not here on the river. The young, newly-trained animal had suddenly alerted on the scent he'd picked up on, right over the side of the boat. But they were on a small boat on the Fox River, and rocking the boat was a no-no. Even with life vests on, no one wanted to go fight the swift current of the Fox, and certainly not Officer Holley, a lieutenant with the Illinois Department of Natural Resources.

Luke imagined that Scout, too, would be pissed at himself should he capsize the boat. Part of the dog's extensive training was how *not* to capsize the lousy little boat the department provided for water search and rescue, or in this case, water recovery of a corpse belonging to a missing young teen.

"Just you try pulling a bloated corpse onto that g'damn postage-stamp sized boat," Luke had said to his desk-jockey, bean-counting counterpart at the office the day before. At the back of the boat today, the bean counter himself, having decided he was ready for some action, sat with both hands white-knuckling the sides of the boat. He did so with both hands each time Scout shook the tub. The overweight Dave Stuart looked as if he wanted off the boat and onto dry land hours ago.

Takes time to find a body under water, Dave,' Luke assured him. "Sometimes takes days, sometimes the person or persons are never found at all. Then some days you get lucky, and you get a calm, no-wind day, and your dog's well-trained, and bingo, a fella like Scout here takes your right to the cadaver."

"Just amazes me how he can sniff odors from thirty or forty feet under water," replied Dave.

"Well, yeah, you gotta consider the depth of the dead man, what's laying over top of him, like rocks, branches, whatever, if he's down there inside a car, if there's blood."

"Scout's onto something," replied Dave. "Hope this is it."

"We got an hour of light left, maybe. We can drop the grappling hook, go fishing, see what we get *holt-of*."

"Or we can come back tomorrow in better light." Dave pointed in the general direction of the sky. The light horizon had shrunk to a narrow squint, and Dave had a point, as nightfall was coming down, a dropping curtain on a darkened theater.

"We leave now, it's going to cost your precious budget that much more, Dave."

"I get that, but-but hell, man, it's getting darker'n hell and kind of spooky out here."

"They don't call it the deep woods for nothin', Dave."

"I 'magine not."

"OK, we go and come back tomorrow mornin', but hey, buddy, by then, you understand, all the conditions will've changed." Luke began making moves that said they were leaving, but Dave, considering things, asked, "Hold on, whataya mean?"

"I mean, time we get back, even if we could locate this exact spot, guess what? We can't depend on Scout alerting again."

"Really? Why not?"

"Maybe he's got nothing to sniff. Maybe the wind's up, or if the current's got *holt-of* the dead guy below."

"*Hmmm* … yeah, I see, and it'd cost the taxpayers big time," Dave said, sighing and frowning. "I'd as soon have the search done-done, buddy, tonight, kaput. Go home with a feeling of accomplishment."

"Accomplishment, eh?" Luke questioned.

"Sure, why not? Bring the deceased back to family for proper burial, respect the remains, all that."

"And suppose it's the family that wanted the deceased down under, below and forgotten?" Luke posed? "County coroner finds poison, ligature marks, blunt force trauma, whatever, then someone gets hunted down by the detectives. Either way, I get a sense of accomplishment. My job — recovery — done proper."

"Just not so sure I want it — the body — lying at my feet here in this tub in the dark is all." Dave sniveled.

Luke chuckled at this. "In all the thirteen years I've been doing black water dives and cadaver recoveries, Dave, I've never had not one of the corpses grab *holt-of* me."

"Yeah, but I've heard your stories, Luke. How even though you know — you know precisely — what you are looking for on a dive, when the corpse's face comes up into your face out of the murky depths, that it startles hell out of you."

"Well sure it does! It's like seeing a well-preserved ghost, all white as a sheet, coming at you. Like they have that last bit of life despite days in the water, and they're grabbing for you, like as if they're thinking hard about hugging you and kissing you and holding on hard to you 'cause you are *life* in pitch darkness. Hell it's like they wanna switch places with you, or something screwy like that."

"Transmigraton of souls," muttered Dave, pushing his glasses up his nose.

"Say what?"

"Switching out your soul for theirs. It's called transmigration … of souls. Some ancient Hindi seers talk about how — "

"No shit. They got a name for it? Where'd you hear 'bout that shit, Dave?"

"Read it somewhere."

"Yeah, that's right, you read a lot, I hear." Luke rolled his eyes.

Scout rocked the boat again, growing more agitated, his nose atwitter with sniffing now. Sniff-sniff-sniffing the air over the side of the small boat, idle above the odor of the cadaver, which must be lifting like a fog that only the dog could detect.

Scout started barking, which was another no-no for a trained, professional sniffer. Scout was not only trained on cadaver odors; he was also trained as a drug sniffer, and he could sniff out ailments in people as well, ailments from diabetes to cancer.

"Stop that noise, Scout! What in tarnation's got into you, boy?" Luke admonished the dog, and the boat balanced out, the shimmy calming long before Dave did.

Luke ushered Scout to the other side of the boat, and he calmly dropped the grappling hook on its chain. As he had earlier dropped the anchor, Luke took care not to work the hook anywhere near the anchor chain.

"Wish I had more time to get out here for fun and fishing," Dave said, one hand on the silent motor that he nervously patted as if it were a fat ham hock. This, while the current played with the boat, twirling it left, right, back again like a fishing bobber. "*Hafta* find a calmer section than this though."

"That's for sure. It's like … as if we're overhead of a vortex or something, and it might be getting stronger … "

"Hardly enough room in the boat for us, Scout, and a full-grown adult teenage cadaver." Dave lit a camp lantern to inspect the space along the keel. "So roomy," he jokingly muttered.

The person they'd come for was a teen who'd gone missing, along with his car, the night of the prom. A young man who was a star on the wrestling team and the football field at Jefferson High, named Trace Fuller. He was a handsome, wholesome kid who likely had fallen asleep at the wheel when going over the Fox River Bridge near Round Lake. Broken beams told the story. The Fox River current told the rest of the tale, as so far, nothing of the car or the boy had been located.

Luke missed his usual partner as Dave, like the dog, wouldn't shut up, and his remarks were getting on Luke's nerves. Dave was saying, "They raise kids on milk these days. They grow 'em bigger'n NBA stars nowadays. Foot size alone is like a 13 or 14 even. Hell, his toes will be in your face, Luke, and his head in mine."

"Dave, Dave, Dave, shut up! I was kidding about haulin' the boy onto the boat. We don't do it that way, not since Smithers turned over his boat, motor in the sky, losing his dog and a corpse to the current, and almost drowning his partner."

"Oh, I heard about that. Awful. Lost the body, department sued over it; the suit was settled. Cost was substantial."

There was silence for a moment, as Luke worked the chains to the grappling hook, until he felt something solid below take hold. Could I be that lucky, he wondered …? "About twenty-six or seven feet below, be my guess. He musta got clear of the car. Likely drowned before he could get to the surface."

"You got him hooked, for real?"

"Feels right, yeah, got the hooks into something." Luke slowly began tugging at it. "Got 'im, I think, hope."

Luke's senses, his instincts, were almost as strong and as good as Scout's. At the same time that Luke was thinking it so, he realized the dog was cowering in the bow of the boat now … a dog afraid of something. He'd never seen Scout behave this way. It disturbed Luke, but he had no idea what it could mean, except to say that Scout might well have to be drummed out of the service unless Luke fudged this night's report.

"So then, Lucky Luke, how do you get the body to shore then?" asked Dave, pulling Luke's attention from Scout and what was on the end of the grappling hook.

"You read a lot, Dave. Figure it out."

"Oh my god. You mean *Old Man and The Sea* fashion, don't you."

"No chance this boat's gonna capsize that way."

"Wow, hope the families have no idea. You know, the optics … no matter that he's dead."

"We anchor the corpse securely to the rear gunnels. Don't worry. I got plenty of chain to work with, and no one's the wiser. Gotta work within our means, right, Dave?"

Dave breathed deeply, soured on the work before it'd been done, but he realized he was at the rear of the boat where the body would be attached. They would leave the body in the water and drag it behind the boat. "So, could we maybe exchange places, Luke?"

"It's fine. Come on up front with Scout, and I'll get back with the chain and the motor. How's that?"

"Well, we both know how you like to be in charge." Dave felt a chill wash over him and through him here in the dark, the lantern he'd had still at arm's reach should he need it.

Luke read Dave's body language, the shiver in particular, along with his features, cut in half as they were by the lantern light. A gentle rain had come softly on. The rain made curtained shadows of the trees on the distant shore. Darkness itself had come on hard as clouds covered moon and stars; this hinted the rain and the shadows were here to stay. They were in for a mild but steady soaking. It had Luke taking off his life vest.

Dave suddenly gasped and pointed and said, "I see the body. There!"

Luke looked out to where Dave pointed, doubtful as he felt the tug of the chain resisting him, the weight of either a tree branch of a body coming up. "For a moment, though, Luke too thought he saw something in the water, but it was just a passing log painted black by the night. Another rain shadow.

"Shoulda gone into some easier line of work, Dave. You don't really have the stomach for this, but I respect your giving it a try — getting out from behind that desk."

They made the shaky, wobbly crisscross position exchange, and the disturbance seemed to get Scout barking again, and again Luke shouted at the dog, saying, "Shut your trap, dog!"

Suddenly, at the same moment, without putting any further effort into hauling up the grappling hook with it prize attached, the prize bobbed up to the surface like a balloon that had been inflated, and there it floated alongside the boat. This was no shadow. This was a bloated, large body that could be taken for the missing teen.

"Bloated all to hell, he is," Luke said to Dave, who'd jumped inwardly on seeing the unnaturally chalk-white skin and waving hair and flailing limbs all decked out in a ridiculously soaked tuxedo.

"Fuckin' prom night," muttered Luke, who felt relief that Scout and he had accomplished this thing here and now, as if blessed, the moon suddenly darted from the clouds overhead and illuminated the catch.

Luke said, "Now I wanna get me home. Hell, Scout and me, we ain't ate since sunup."

"Well, me neither," complained Dave.

"There ain't no golden arches on the Fox River, but you know, Dave, the thought gives me an idea. You come out here with a 'sandwich boat,' you know like a mobile diner, say like on the weekends, bet you could make a good buck on baloney sandwiches."

"Fishing makes a man hungry for sure."

Scout again broke training, barking anew. Why's Scout still barking, Luke wondered even as he clipped the chains to the rear of the boat, securing the young running back who'd died so suddenly that he hardly knew what'd hit him.

That's when Luke looked back at Dave, and he watched, semi-mesmerized as a fog enveloped first Scout at mid-boat, then the fog covered Dave at the bow.

For a moment, all Luke saw was Dave's eyes growing larger, until the eyes were huge in the semi-glow of the lantern. Something was terrifying Dave, making him shiver, and Luke caught a glimpse of it in Dave's eyes, for in those eyes, Luke saw the mirrored reflection of a whiter fog.

This fog had risen from the rear of the boat to envelope Luke. In fact, the sudden supposed river fog had lifted off the surface, rather than roiling down from the air.

White fog had come from the river where the corpse bobbed behind the boat, behind Lucky Luke. From the water, from the corpse, it originated ... this kinetic fog ... and it was already infiltrating Luke's body before he realized it wanted him. The white kinetic fog was busily filling his body like water filling a vessel. Filling him with its essence, while Luke's own soul was being squeezed and tugged, pushed and pulled from his body. No room in him for his essence and that of the fog both.

In just seconds the whole thing happened; Luke found himself face down in the water and feeling helplessly blob-like, unable to gather strength. He was also being tugged by the boat, as the motor had come to life. Forcing his head up, eyes of the corpse blinking, Lucky Luke watched the boat with Scout, Dave, and the soul of the dead teenager, racing off for shore. This, while dragging the body, with Luke inside it, behind the roaring motor. Luke realized Dave had weighed anchor, as Scout surely hadn't that talent, so Dave wasn't near as frozen as he'd appeared.

Luke felt the snap and tug of the cold grappling hooks where they'd caught the corpse's ribs — now his ribs. He smelled the decay now as it was his own decay flowing into the current, knowing no cadaver dogs were going to save him. These thoughts filled his mind like acid, even as he caught a glimpse through the rain of the three shadows silhouetted on the boat. Scout now being petted by the dead teen while Dave looked away and toward shore as if his life depended on slapping his foot on solid ground.

Dave, at the bow, had turned to stone, his stare frozen along with his gaping mouth. He had been a witness to a transmigration of souls. The hero of Jefferson High on the ball field knew he wanted Luke's body over either Scout's or Dave's, which made the panicking Luke wonder if he shouldn't be proud at having been the Chosen One.

Had the spirit in the tux chosen wisely because it knew that Lucky Luke got his nickname for his talents as a fisherman or a black water diver? The relationships among the three creatures in the boat had completely altered, and Lucky would never be the same man ever again. The last thing Luke saw before all went black was Scout sniff-sniffing at what had been Luke. Sniffing at the rain shadow soul inside Luke's body. Small comfort, but at least Scout knew the truth. Dave, on the other hand, being human, would doubt everything he saw and felt this night, second-guessing himself into non-belief. This was Luke's last thought before Lucky ran out of luck and all sensation. ■

Robert W. Walker is the author the Bloodscreams *series featuring vampire-hunter Abraham Stroud (available from Bold Venture Press). His award-winning "Inspector Alastair Ransom" historical mysteries —* City for Ransom *(2006),* Shadows In the White City *(2007), and* City of the Absent *(2008) — are published by HarperCollins.*

Meet Abraham Stroud ... Hi-tech vampire-hunter ...

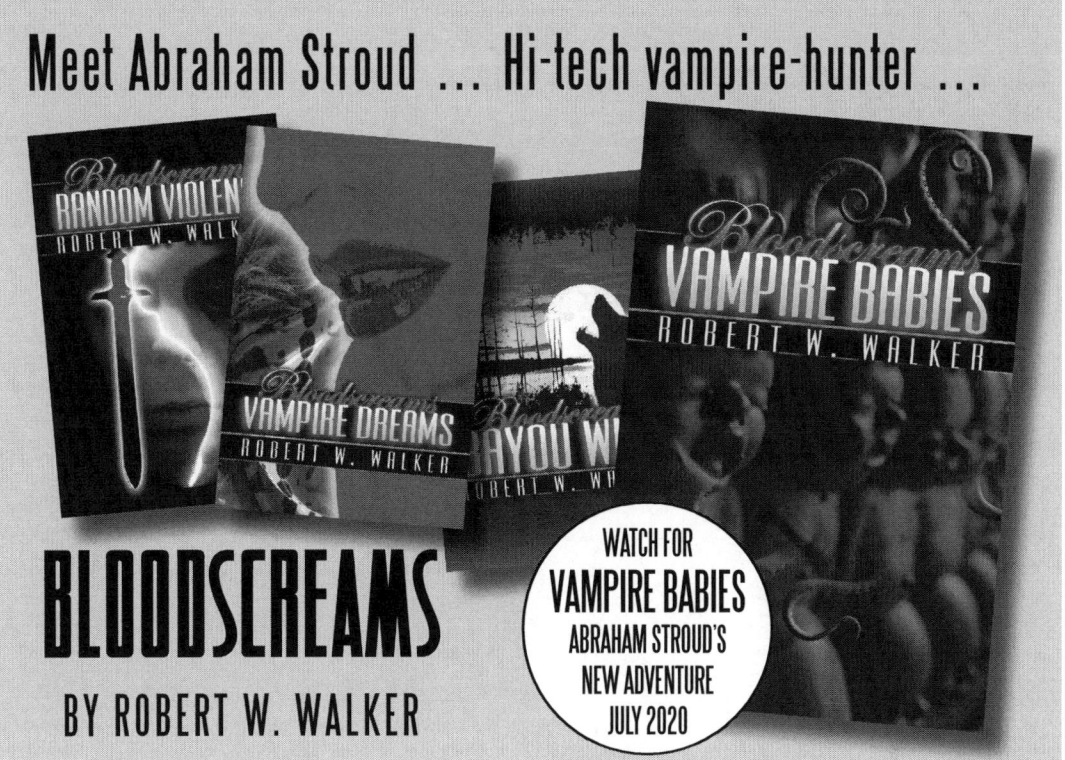

BLOODSCREAMS
BY ROBERT W. WALKER

WATCH FOR **VAMPIRE BABIES** ABRAHAM STROUD'S NEW ADVENTURE JULY 2020

DEGREES OF SEPARATION?

FBI Agent Megan McKenna was eager to prove herself by capturing the notorious "Wishing Well Killer" — until she learned of her personal connection to the culprit!

FBI Agent Megan McKenna makes her debut in the explosive new novel by Megan Phillips Walker

WWW.BOLDVENTUREPRESS.COM

Art: Howard Simpson

GIVE 'EM HELL, HELEN

Adam McFarlane

THE car screamed down the road. Gravel and a haze of grit flung up in its wake. The low thrum meant a belt had snapped, slapping the cylinder block in a continuous drone. The engine was on fire. As white smoke streamed from the fan-shaped exhaust pipe, black smog spilled out the hood's ventilating louvers.

The driver's leather gauntlets spun the wood-rimmed steering wheel as she tried to keep all four wheels on the road. Her cap clung tightly to her skull, while stands of straw-colored hair whipped out from under it by the wind.

The car was painted with ivory-colored enamel. A black circle on the side inscribed with a stylized P — for Pegasus — was meant to resemble a race number. Muck clung to the mudguards and running boards. Dirt smeared chrome hinges and handles, and spoiled the car's cream palette. The radiator grill was discolored and dented. Protected by wire mesh, oversized headlights looked out over a double bumper of wavy chrome tube.

Beside her in the two-seat cockpit, the relief driver tapped a glass dial; its needle continued to waver. Oil leaked in his footwell.

"I don't think we're going to make it," she shouted over the noise.

The relief driver clung to the dashboard. Since they lacked a windshield and roof, wind pushed against his face. He pointed to the horizon. "There's a gas station. Stop there."

Farmlands stretched to the horizon, surfaces of brown and green sloping into a river valley and over gently rolling hills. Planted crops barely broke above the ground. Pole to pole, American Telephone and Telegraph wires followed the road like a child re-tracing a connect-the-dots. Burma Shave messages and dueling billboards for Roosevelt and Landon whizzed past.

Wind flapped the driver's long white scarf and her straw-blonde hair. She blinked through her aviator goggles, then she nodded.

The filling station had a crenellated rooftop with towers at its corners. Matching the insignia above each gas pump, the building was topped by a yellow wooden crown. It was an Auto King.

The car rolled up to the first pump and came to a rumbling, juddering, furious halt.

Wiping gloved fingers across the dust coating her goggles, she managed to rub the fine particles into an opaque smudge. "Dag nabbit!"

An attendant stepped out of the castle. "Welcome to Auto King, home of the — "

"We're not interested. Can you check the tire pressure and water level?" the relief driver said.

The attendant was an older man with little hair apart from gray whiskers. His overalls were streaked with grease. "Sure thing, sir. Wipe your windshield and wash the windows, too?" he said, glancing at the car. It had no windshield nor windows. "Oh right, never mind."

"Thanks, Bobby," the driver said, noticing the name embroidered on the attendant's shirt. "My name's Helen and his is Jim. Do you have a telephone?"

"Yes, ma'am," he said, thumbing over his shoulder to the building.

With her goggles, scarf, and leather gloves, Helen looked more like an aviator than a driver to Bobby. As they disembarked from the cockpit, he watched them clamber over the sides (the Pegasus had no doors). She looked only twenty years old. He'd never seen a woman driver before, much less a woman racer.

"I don't think we're in Kansas anymore, Toto," she said. Taking off her cap, her long hair flowed freely. Blonde strands descended to her shoulders. Her blue eyes were pale, and they matched her light complexion.

"We haven't made it to Kansas yet; this is still Illinois," Jim responded as they walked into the filling station. Nearly forty years old, white strands salted his black hair.

Inside the station were maps, glass soda pop bottles, and batteries. The smell of brewing coffee wafted in the air. Cans of sludge solvent and grease were stacked in perfect pyramids. Mounted behind a wire rack that offered free promotional road atlases and lick-and-save Auto King discount stamps, a black telephone hung with its cord dangling like a tail.

Jim fetched the receiver, "Operator? I'd like to place a person-to-person call."

Bobby stepped back into the room. "You don't mind me asking, mister, you paying cash or you setting up a weekly account for credit?"

"Cash," he answered then looked at the telephone. "Yes, New York." Jim gave the operator the number, then paused. "Hello, Sam? This is Jim. Yeah, we're in — " he turned and looked at Bobby.

"Belle Plaine."

"Belle Plaine, Illinois. We're pissing oil, our radiator is busted, and something's screwy with our engine thermometer. I'm thinking a new head gasket, but maybe more copper fins and fresh brass tubing, too?"

A radio sat on the counter beside the cash register. Dust dulled the radio's varnish. An orchestra's waltz faded in and out, peppered with static. Through the wavering transmission, an announcer's voice broke in for a news bulletin, "Be on the lookout for Stefano Pavoni. He is believed to be armed and extremely dangerous."

Bobby walked out to the gas pumps.

Helen was outside stretching her limbs, feeling the sun on her face.

"I hope the powder room was to your satisfaction?"

"Oh, yes," she said, bending in a less un-lady-like posture.

In the distance, church steeples and low brick buildings clustered together. Farther away, a grain elevator, a water tower, and a line of windbreak trees bumped the horizon.

"Where'd y'all come from, if you don't mind me asking?"

"This morning? Chicago. But I'm from Baltimore, originally."

Bobby gave the car another look. With the hood up, its twelve-cylinder crank case was visible. The Pegasus was a locomotive on wheels.

"You're not one of the Detroit Cup racers, are you?" he asked.

She smiled. "In fact, we are. We started in New York last week."

The Detroit Cup was "The Seven City Race Across America," from New York to Philadelphia, along the Great Lakes — Cleveland, Detroit, and Chicago — down to St. Louis, then across the West to Los Angeles.

"That makes you … "

Nodding, she said, "Helen Mackay."

Mackay Motors was American's ninth largest automobile manufacturer, and the Pegasus was the prototype for a new design. The company's owner, Joseph Mackay, wanted to show it off in a coast-to-coast auto race: the Detroit Cup. Mackay made cars outside of Detroit like Marmon, Auburn, and Pierce-Arrow did. But the old man wanted to sell the cars, the factories, and the technology to Detroit, the way General Motors bought Opel and Vauxhall or like Chrysler bought the Dodge Brothers. Parading down Woodward Avenue and on the front page of the *Detroit News* and the *Detroit Free Press* would catch Henry Ford's attention, he hoped.

"Why not include Pittsburgh? It's practically on the way from Philly to Cleveland." Bobby asked.

"There are no people in Pittsburgh," Helen said.

"Then what about Boston? Boston has more people than St. Louie."

"That would make it The Eight City Race Across America."

"What's wrong with The Eight City Race?"

"Eight isn't a number, seven is. Besides, there are more people in New York City — lots more — so it's better to start in New York. Going up to Boston from New York then down to Philadelphia would look daft."

Five cars had revved their engines before a crowd of hundreds on the steps of the New York Public Library. To launch the race, movie star Jim Taylor fired a gold-plated revolver. Each car sprang to life, but abided by the speed limit. Leaving Manhattan over the Brooklyn Bridge in single file, a slight breeze allowed a delusion of zooming over the East River.

"Here comes the cavalry," Jim said, stepping out as Bobby withdrew into the filling station.

They came in two cars, sedans with extra parts filling the empty seats. Three men in boots, breeches, and denim shirts. Luckily, they were less than an hour's drive from the nearest Mackay Motors dealership. Helen's father owned nearly one hundred.

"Smoke?" Helen asked, joining Jim under the station's eaves. He opened up his cigarette case. Like the Pegasus, they were beat from the road. A thunderstorm had drenched the open cockpit last night, leaving them cold, sleepless, and shivering for hours. Now they stood, reviving with cups of coffee and sharing a cigarette.

"I hope they don't smell the puke," Helen said. She had become sick out of Chicago but opted not to stop. She leaned as far as she could out of the cockpit, yet the half-digested slop caught the wind and wound up in her hair and spread across the trunk.

She handed the cigarette, half-smoked, to Jim. He took a drag. "Radio says Stefano Pavoni is out this way."

"The gangster?" Helen asked.

He nodded.

"We're a long way from Jersey."

"If he gets to Kansas City, he'll be safe." Kansas City's crooked police didn't arrest gangsters who stayed law-abiding within city limits.

Bobby came out with a written bill. Jim took his wallet out and counted out dollars. Had the pump jockey, he wondered, jacked up the price? Attendants were often paid on commission, and commissions would be low in the middle of nowhere.

"What's that they're taking out?" Helen asked, nodding toward the men.

"The radiator's getting replaced," Jim said.

She pondered for a moment. The Detroit Cup promoted cars for the American people — cars that regular folks wanted to buy, cars that didn't need expensive repairs. The rules forbid major parts being changed during the race. To guarantee that, each major part was stamped before race day.

She asked, "Are we disqualified?"

Jim shook his head. "Replace the part now, send the broken one by train to Denver, then once we get there, switch it back."

"What if someone finds out?"

"All that matters is that we roll into L.A. before anyone else. And since the Federal Motors car got lost outside of Toledo, we're in good shape."

Watching him, Helen blinked.

"The Pegasus will make barrels of money. They'll have to sue Old Joe before he admits anything and, while the shysters bicker in court, we'll drive up and down both coasts, selling these tin wagons."

The team checked the gasoline dipstick then filled the tank. The red needle on the pump slowly turned around the gallon dial.

"What about the Nike?" Helen asked.

"Drove off an embankment and broke their axle."

The repair crew added Solarene motor lubricant. With a supercharger fit for a Boeing, the Pegasus engine ran hot.

"So, we're cheating?"

Jim shrugged. "We're winning."

The driver's manual would recommend Solarene over other oil brands, provided they won and put the Pegasus in mass production. Solarene was good to the last drop.

"Was nobody worried that I would find out?"

He took a long drag on the cigarette,

dropped it to dirt, and ground it out. "They don't really care, Helen."

They don't really care? She went to all the best cafes and restaurants. *Photoplay* had shown her at a movie premier. She was honorary president of the Kings County Animal Welfare Society and donated regularly to the New York Infirmary for Indigent Women and Children. Serious people gave her serious attention — not least of all, her father. She was the daughter of one of the richest people in New York.

"Well, they should." She sniffed. "They don't call me Give-'em-Hell-Helen for nothing."

Jim put a new cigarette to his lips. "They don't call you Give-'em-Hell-Helen … Helen."

She laughed. "Sure they do. When I'm on the other side of a door or in the hallway, sometimes I hear people in Daddy's offices say it. They don't think I hear, but I do."

After lighting the next cigarette, Jim said, "It's not 'Give them Hell' they're saying."

"Of course it is." She put her hands on her hips. "What do you think they're saying?"

"Give-*him*-Hell-Helen."

"Him who?"

"Who else? Your dad."

Helen froze. Jim transformed before her eyes. Ever since he guided her first tour of Mackay Motors' factory, Jim had been like an uncle to her. He brought her lollipops as a girl and cigarettes as an adult. Old Joe's right-hand man, he was liaison to the design team and the test driver on every prototype.

Now, he was her father's henchman. Doing the dirty deeds Daddy wouldn't admit to, she realized, including bamboozling his own daughter.

She saw Bobby following the conversation through the window. He averted his eyes, then he fumbled with the radio dials. The broadcast machine's announcer called the time, updated the news about Stefano Pavoni, and returned listeners to a ballroom of music somewhere far, far away.

"What if we didn't finish the race?"

Jim cocked his head. "We'll finish the race, it's just a question of placing first or second. Considering the Choctaw lost six hours from the — "

"I mean, what if we just quit?"

"Quit?" He stated, raising the question with his eyebrows.

"What if we went after Stefano Pavoni, instead?" she said, and gestured to the Pegasus. "It's the only thing that can catch him."

A breeze passed through, mussing their hair and carrying the scent of tilled earth. The mechanics continued to tinker and wrestle with the steel guts under their car's hood.

Chewing on his lip, Jim was lost in thought. "I don't know if that's exactly legal. They don't round up posses anymore like in the movies. It's not *like* the chief of police would just deputize us — "

"No, the city police don't deputize. But the land along the highway is the county sheriff's domain."

Bobby stopped pretending not to hear. "You want I should call him?"

Helen nodded, and Jim walked inside to the phone. While Bobby placed the call, Jim sat beside him.

The team drove off without a word. Of course they did, Helen thought. If they never talked to her or Jim, they could admit honestly that they never talked to any mechanics about engine parts. If asked who replaced the engine, she would say she didn't know.

Jim held out the phone receiver. "He wants to talk to you, Helen."

When Helen took the phone, Jim stood under the eaves and looked out over the horizon.

She spoke into the phone. "Well, I don't know about that, Sheriff. Yes, um … but how do you expect us to catch him if we abide by the speed limit? Yes, uh-huh. Then I swear to abide by all the laws of the state of Illinois except for posted speed limits. So-help-me-God."

Bobby went into the station and brought out a rifle, holding it with both hands at the barrel. He presented it to Jim.

"A Browning Automatic?" Jim said. It had a pistol grip in front of a black walnut stock. He lifted it to his shoulder. It was heavy — nearly 20 pounds, he guessed — but the barrel's sight posts were perfectly aligned.

"The magazines screw in and hold twenty rounds. I've got a whole shelf full, if you like."

"I'd like, all right," he said, continuing to look though the sights. It was a hell of a lot more firepower than he had at the Hindenburg Line. And now there were a lot fewer people to shoot. He looked at Helen.

She returned his gaze.

"You know what I say to Joseph Mackay and the American people and Stefano Pavani?"

Shaking her head, she said, "No, what?"

"Give them Hell, Helen."

With a wide grin, she jumped into the cockpit. Jim followed on the passenger side. She released the brake, opened the choke, and flipped the battery switch. *I'll be taken seriously after all*, Helen told herself.

"Listen for us on the radio," she said to Bobby, then tugged the ignition lever.

Using the information the sheriff had said over the telephone, they crisscrossed the roads. Stefano Pavoni's car was a convertible Morris sedan, greener than a dollar bill. It strayed from the highways to avoid police roadblocks. But the dusty fog it raised on dirt roads made it easy to find.

Jim stood astride the running board, his boots firm against its treads.

In the green Morris were Angus "Gat" Murphy, Abner Shapiro, and Gat Murphy's girlfriend Chloe, plus her green wrap trailing in the wind.

With one eye closed and one eye squinting at its target, Jim aimed for tires. The dust fogged his aim too much — he hit rear lights and the trunk. The bootleggers had equal luck throwing hot lead at them, fouling wide left and right. Jim was impressed; some of his shots merely dented steel and cracked extra-thick glass in the green Morris. He could aim for the passengers, but that wouldn't be as fun.

Helen clutched the steering wheel with her leather gloves. Although her jaw was clenched, dimples dented the ends of her lips. And her eyes scrunched up, but they glittered with excitement. Her heart raced harder as she pressed the gas pedal hard. She hoped Jim was hanging on. With the Pegasus, she'd drive her way onto the front pages of the newspaper, without playing into her daddy's corporate machinations. She was going to write her own headlines. She let out a war whoop and smashed the pedal to the floor.

Watch for more
Tales of the Black Island Tavern
by Adam McFarlane
in future issues of
Pulp Adventures!

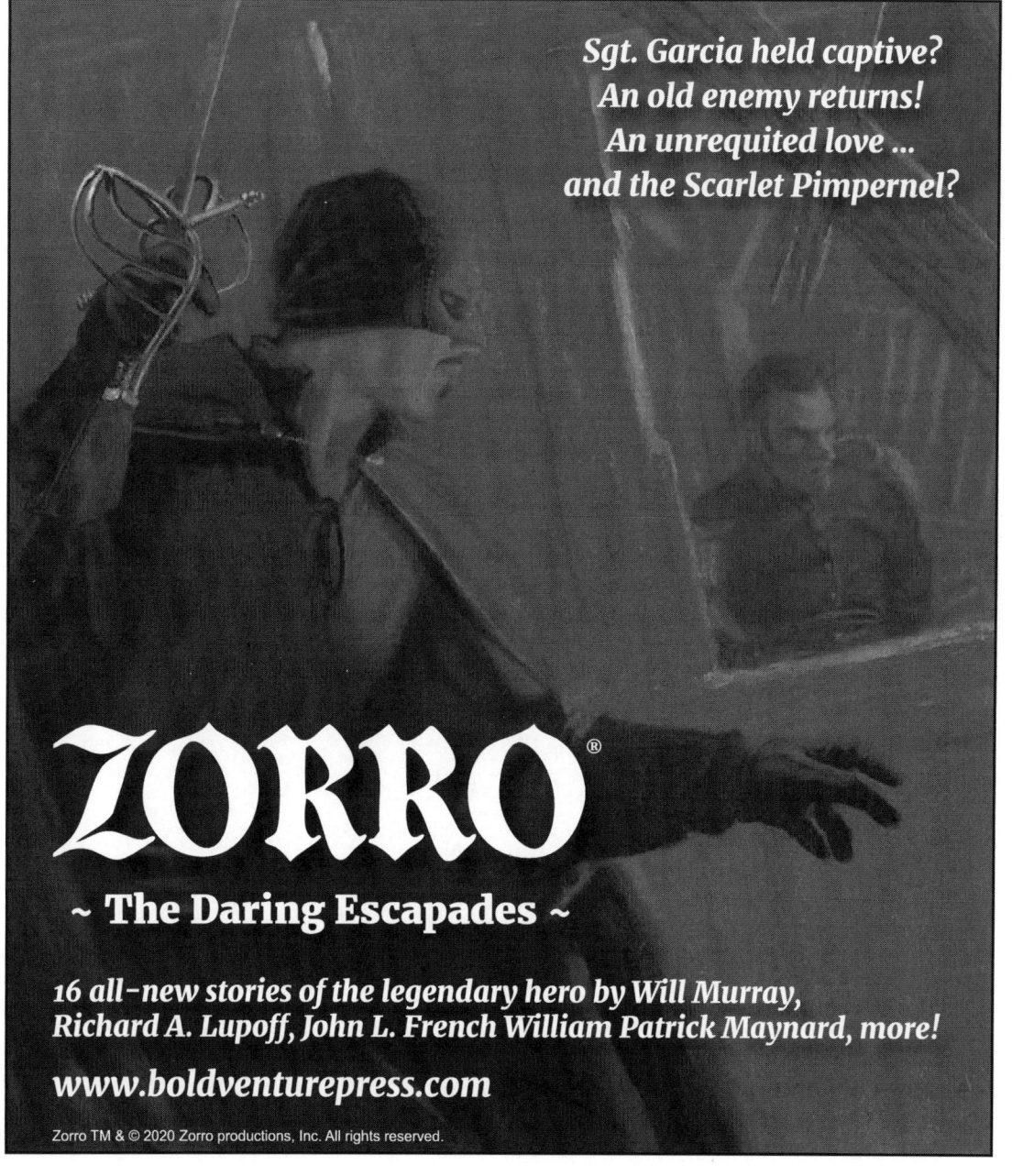

Sgt. Garcia held captive?
An old enemy returns!
An unrequited love ...
and the Scarlet Pimpernel?

ZORRO®
~ The Daring Escapades ~

16 all-new stories of the legendary hero by Will Murray, Richard A. Lupoff, John L. French William Patrick Maynard, more!

www.boldventurepress.com

Zorro TM & © 2020 Zorro productions, Inc. All rights reserved.

The Occurrence of the KALI CURSE

By TEEL JAMES GLENN

*Hola! Musketeers
Mother of Cities to me,
For I was born in her gate,
Between the palms and the sea,
Where the world-end steamers wait.*
— Kipling on 'Bombay'

Prologue

Manderson began it all and set in motion the circumstances that brought this curse on us all.

It started innocently enough. He was in from the Crimea on leave to visit family in Bombay just after the rainy season. He, Horne and I met at the officer's club just down the street from the New Post Office to begin the night of drinking and boasting.

Toby Horne was a solid fellow from the royal engineers assigned to the Bandra Reclamation. Tall and blonde with a substantial mustache, that he continually brushed with an absentminded gesture, he was from Kent back home and had been out here for five years. He bloody well hated it.

George Manderson was with the Horseguard, as was I and was dark enough to be a Frenchie. He had been seconded to the corps of the Bengal Pioneers and was not terribly happy with that appointment.

For myself, I had been sent by Doctor Argent to serve with The Governor General's office as a liaison to the police force of the city. I was an old hand in Bombay born of parents who had been stationed there. I considered myself practically an Anglo-Indian and had none of the problems with the various cultures of my second home.

I had met the fellows while studying in England and we had been nicknamed "the three inseparables' by many of the tavern keepers and not a few of the ladies of that area. Our postings had only been a minor interruption in our bachelor party lives.

Whenever we three chaps were near any city, we found a way to get together and uphold our legend.

That night in October we had started drinking at the officer's club and then went a-wandering toward the Mahim district. It was a close-built area of simple people, not the usual haunts of officers on the prowl for a good time, but we three captains had tired of the usual haunts.

"I tell you Stone," Manderson said to me as we walked down a narrow street that bordered the Mithi River that drains into Mahim Creek. "I heard it from old Sanders that this Blue Mongoose Club is the best time he ever had."

The Creek drained into the Bay and formed the border between the city and suburbs. The outer cafes were our destination, more exotic even than the bazaars of the inner city where rumor had it of pleasures even we experienced debauchers had not seen.

"I think we should just stay in the district and drink ourselves into a bloody coma, boys," Horne said. "All this walking is bad for my reputation; I should be astride a great charger at the head of a brigade!"

We laughed at that; he was the worst rider of the bunch of us at school.

"You have no reputation worth saving," Manderson said, "but we can build a solid legend at this Blue Mongoose that you can spend a goodly number of years living down, eh wot?"

We laughed again — we laughed often when we were together and walked into the gloom looking for a new adventure.

Mahim had originally been one of the seven islands that made up old Bombay itself. Since the Raj had been filling the bays and repairing the causeways to improve sanitation after the plagues the city had been growing by leaps and bounds.

To our left was Mahim Bay part of the Arabian Sea. We moved toward the Worli area and into a quarter where Anglo-Indian faces were rarer.

I know my friends were only interested in the next drink, but I have to say that I reveled in the spicy smells and the very ambiance of the native streets. I had missed it while in England, which may be why I adapted so quickly to service with Doctor Argent with his many Eastern ways. I thought of myself as almost more Indian than English at times in all that, though I would never say it to my friends.

Like Mister Kipling, whom I had met once several years ago when he had moved back to England from Vermont, the age and wisdom of that dark sub-continent seemed deeper in many ways than Europe's. I never professed to understand much f that mystery, perhaps my very Scottishness prevented me from doing so, but I did try.

After the events of that night, I am not sure I ever could understand those dark mysteries no matter how much time I spend with the Doctor.

The usual swarm of turbaned locals moved around us, their eyes circumspect in their glances, not daring to meet the eyes of their conquerors.

Most in that district were Sea Kolis, the ancient fisher race that had first inhabited the islands which had become Bombay. They were not the lowest of the castes, not untouchable, but still low enough that we had corrupted their name to coolie as a euphemism for manual workers. They worshiped the goddess Ekveera at the Karla caves, Malavli, Lonavla. Some said she was an aspect of Kali which made many of the government suspicious of them and that wariness kept many in the uniform of the Empire from the district.

We were quite the spectacle, and as we progressed down the narrow streets, we could hear the murmur of voices from the shadows. We countered by singing an old Scottish ditty called "Hadrian's Folly." The Horseguards favored the melody in many a pub though we were probably a bit off tune without beer tankards in our hands to even out our voices.

> *The rumble of their footsteps shook the earth like 'quakes*
> *Their voices called for horrid death and made the heavens shake*
> *The legions of the wolf twin state are set upon our shores*
> *Now we the blue clad warriors will meet them all in wars*
>
> *From Highland keeps we'll thunder down*
> *No mercy in our cry*
> *To drive the 'ruders from our home*
> *Or know the reason why*
> *And if they offer terms to us*
> *Or bargain for our thrall*
> *We'll strike at them thrice fiercely back—*
> *And make'm build a wall!*

"Careful, chaps! I'm dangerously close to sobering up," Horne said as we finished a second chorus and walked down another twisting byway. We were all staggering like wheat in a stiff wind and I doubt if any of us were really capable of sobering up for days, but I knew how Horne felt. The adventure was fading from the trip one should not have to work so hard at having a good time!

"There it is, my brothers!" Manderson pointed to a cut-out of a mongoose that hung as a sign outside an otherwise unremarkable door in a narrow alley.

It was not a very appealing place, nor particularly noteworthy in appearance. Just another doorway in a sea of dark portals lining the brick and waddle street. As there were paving stones, it was not the poorest section to be sure, but I heard no gay music nor saw any revelers pouring forth from the doorway to mark it as the night-spot it was supposed to be.

"Not much better than my lodgings in Brighton," Horne muttered, "and a darn sight gloomier; I think Sanders was having a go at you, George."

"No, no!" Manderson insisted, "He would not steer a fellow wrong; let's go inside. I'm sure it will be fine."

"After all this walking," Horne muttered, "it had better be more than fine."

The darkness had descended on the city with little mitigation from the faint moonlight, so all around us the shapes of locals were little more than smudges of black on black. What little light spilled from the shutters of windows served only to add to the mystery of those around us rather than reveal details.

I bumped into one of the shapes and heard a mumbled, "Excuse, please *Sahib*," from him. Like most Indian's the shape was not as tall as I, but I could discern little else.

"My fault entirely, sir," I replied.

It was as if my speaking triggered an avalanche for suddenly forms descended on us out of the darkness and I saw a stray beam of light slash across an upraised knife blade.

"Up lads" I yelled, "cutthroats!"

My fellows shook their alcohol-induced lethargy with amazing rapidity. We all cried out our battle call "*Hola!*" and plunged into the half dozen thugs that had decided we were easy prey. We were not half so drunk as they had hoped and in a writhing sea of arms, legs and fists we were a solid mass of fury.

We had fought so often side by side, both on the playing fields at rugby, in battle and at taverns across the empire, so that the poor fool cutpurses had not nearly the advantage they had hoped.

In short order the brigands retreated at a run and we three backed against a wall to assess our conditions.

"Not the lively time I had hoped for," Manderson said. He had a bloody nose and a cut on his tunic sleeve that, fortunately, had not caught flesh.

"You always did have friends in low place, George," Horne said. He was relatively unscathed save for a slight bruise on his cheek and his hair askew. His cap was gone as well.

I was untouched by the violence and had even managed to secure a curved dagger from one of the attackers as a souvenir. "I say we've come this far, chaps, let's see if this Mongoose is all its advertised to be!"

'Here, here!" they both rejoined and we turned to head for the door of the café.

"The *sahibs* should heed omens," a thin voice floated to us out of the darkness.

We spun as one to face what we supposed to be a fresh attack. Instead, a small figure tottered out of the blackness. He was indistinguishable from thousands of beggars that swarmed the streets of the city. A rail thin arm protruded from layers of cloth that were of indeterminate color and rough texture.

"Get off you sodding beggar," Manderson said. He looked as if he was going to strike the old man but the ragged figure did not flinch even before I moved to stay George's blow.

"Is not charity one of the cardinal virtues of even your religion, *sahib*?" The old man said. He had stepped into the center of the street now and the moon chose that moment to slither from behind a cloud to illuminate the beggar.

His eyes were startlingly white against his dark brown skin, the pupils tiny black spots that seemed to swirl with power. I could see the red dot clearly on his forehead beneath the twisted cloth of his head covering.

"Oh, leave him be, George," Horne said, "He's just looking for a meal." Horne fished in his pocket and drew out a few Rupees.

"May you be blessed," the old mendicant muttered as the coins dropped into his wrinkled palm. "And may the vengeance of *Ekveera Devi* be lightest on the most just of you all."

"That's a ruddy odd blessing," Horne

said as we walked away from the old man toward the door to the café.

"All these bloody wogs are ruddy odd," Manderson said with a sneer. "I can't wait to leave this miserable country."

"Well the beer is good enough," Horne said, "Let's see what this Blue Mongoose of ours has to offer to silence that snarl of yours; I do think you are sobering up!"

I watched my two friends move ahead of me but I kept my gaze back at the old man. He saw me looking and his near toothless grin was somehow eerie. As I gazed at him, he deliberately tossed the Rupees away and then vanished into the darkness of the night with a cackle like a jackal's call.

Chapter One
Like a Cobra to a Mongoose.

When the door to the Blue Mongoose creaked inward, we three were assailed by scents and sounds that were India in all of its mystery and power. Flutes, drums and cymbals sounded out an old *Koli* song I knew from *Narlai Punaw*, the holiday that celebrated the day the winds changed to favor the fishing fleet. *"San aaila go narali punvecha,"* a chorus of voices said as we entered.

We went down a narrow set of steps into a large room that had more the feeling of a cave than a nightclub, with arched spaces that faded off into shadowed alcoves where the patrons were ensconced. A small group of musicians were on a small stage while two women stood before it singing the song in *puja* of the god-sea, calling for good fortune for their boats.

"Welcome to the Blue Mongoose, *sahibs*," a *maitre de* presented himself to us as we reached the bottom of the steps. "If you will follow me, I will find the finest seats in this humble establishment for you."

I saw several staff officers in the shadowed side spaces puffing on hookahs, some of them with female companions. There were many more civilians around the club though unlike many nightclubs there were a number of Indians seated in the room. I noticed there were both Hindu and Moslems there as well, which I found unusual, for the followers of Islam were generally not to found in such places and certainly not in the mixed company of the Hindus.

There were several of the *koli* sub-castes in the serving staff and among the musicians, *Koli kolis, Mahadeo kolis,* and *Suryawanshi kolis*. The Blue Mongoose seemed to be a neutral zone of sorts. I wondered if that was the appeal for Manderson's sapper friend to recommend the place. It seemed hardly enough.

Our host led us to a small table in an alcove across from the musicians. A serving girl appeared as if by magic to take our orders. When she had vanished to fetch our drinks, a hookah and some towels for us to clean up appeared; we relaxed.

"It's a nice enough club, chaps," Horne said, "But I don't see anything special about it."

His voiced doubt seemed a cue for the music to suddenly change, a chant in the *Koli* language of *Maharashtra*. The timbre of the room changed; the air felt abruptly charged with power. The cymbals began to clatter like machine guns and the drums boomed like summer thunder.

"Hallo!" Manderson whispered to me, "This looks promising."

> **The whirling figure held every eye in the room and I found myself holding my breath as she abruptly made a wild spin and a layer of her silk gown flew off.**

He was not wrong.

A dancer stepped out from behind a curtain. Her face was veiled and her form swathed in green and blue patterned silks. Though diaphanous, the silks seemed to reveal more than they concealed implying a lithe form wrapped in the colors of the sea. There were bells on her bare feet and in a latticework along her arms and hands that she caused to tinkle to the beat of the drums.

She paused like a statue of some ancient goddess. Her crossed arms and delicate fingers framed her face where eyes the color of coal blazed. The dancer stood frozen, unmoving save for the liquid undulations of her gown that looked all the more like the ocean embodied.

"Promising is not the half of it," Manderson said. His eyes glowed as he watched her over the rim of a tankard. "I'd like to take a look beneath that veil."

"I'd like to take a peek under those silk skirts," Horne leered. "Now I don't think that walk was so bad."

The woman slid across the floor like liquid fire moving into the room. When she reached the exact center of the club the tone of the chant changed yet again to a lilting tune.

The dark-haired siren began to sway to the music in the most extraordinary fashion alternately appearing to be a living green flame and a crashing wave for her fluidity. The bells on her fingers and feet now sounded in counter point to the musicians bringing to my mind the sound of wind chimes or singing birds.

The whirling figure held every eye in the room and I found myself holding my breath as she abruptly made a wild spin and a layer of her silk gown flew off. The men in the club gasped as one as her long brown legs was revealed.

Her body fulfilled the promise of the silks.

"Your friend undersold this place, George," Horne said, "remind me to send him a case of champagne."

"Rather," I whispered. "Double for me."

The dancer flowed around the room now, her bare feet sliding along the floor as if on a column of air. As she neared our table, I felt the power of her presence and it seemed to me that the temperature of the

---

Stories by Teel James Glenn have appeared in Weird Tales, Mystery Weekly, Spinetingler, Pulp Adventures, Sherlock Holmes Mystery *and other magazines.*

room increased. I know my blood pressure had increased with my pounding heart competing with the tempo of the drums.

There was a scent as well, not a perfume or incense but a smell of the sea and flowers all at once. And a musky something more.

I could see that every man in the room was leaning forward with the same rapt expression on their faces I know I had on mine. Manderson was beside himself, his mouth agape his eyes wide. He had not taken a drink since she began to dance, in fact, I suspect he had barely taken a breath.

The girl seemed to have no bones, her liquid form bending and swaying in ways that were both erotic and sensual. Somehow, while she whirled and writhed, she made eye contact with me so that I felt her eyes were fixed on me. I suspect each man there felt the same faux intimacy with her.

The music changed again and she shed another layer of silk so that her midsection was now revealed and she had a sort of half cape of blue green flowing behind her. Even more startling than her mahogany muscular belly was the pattern printed on the cape; when she snatched up the edges of it and spread her arms to the sides the shape behind her had four arms painted on to it.

"*Ekveera Devi!*" I murmured in a stunned whisper.

"Bloody *Kali,* the killer goddess!" Manderson hissed.

The music became martial then, the tempo violent and her fluid, sensual movement took on a frantic, dangerous aspect. It was riveting in the extreme. My eyes followed her movements in a dizzying pattern so that they soon ached as if I had been staring into the Kashmiri sun.

Horne was entranced, or rather hypnotized by her as most of us were, but Manderson seemed to be angered by her sudden transformation. His agitation increased as her dance continued and she seemed to focus her attention in our direction.

Manderson's breathing became a hissing release of air as he leaned forward to leer at her. I became vaguely aware that my friend was rocking back and forth, his fists balled on his lap. He began to mutter in whispered words "Ruddy wog thugees!"

The dancer had begun to chant along with the drummers and singers "*Ekveera Devi, Kali Kali!*" Over and over. She swayed as if in a trance. Her midnight black eyes bored into us and I felt as if some force were sucking my very soul from me.

I found it hard to breath as if the six arms of the dancer's totem were squeezing around my chest. I began to get dizzy and my vision clouded and burred so that in a red haze it appeared to me as if she truly had multiple arms.

I am going mad, I thought and I tried to force sound from my lips, to yell "stop!" but my throat was paralyzed.

The girl clapped her hands over her head and raised one leg looking suddenly like so many images of Hindu deities. It seemed to trigger something in Manderson, something dark.

He sprang forward from his seat and flew at the girl with his fists raised with an animal cry of anger. Everyone in the room was so stunned by his actions that he was able to tackle her to the ground and begin to strangle her before any of us moved.

"Stop it George!" Horne screamed.

The two of us were upon our friend in ten heartbeats and attempted to pry his hands away from the girl's throat by main strength.

"Let her go!" I yelled in his ear, "What's got into you, George? Stop this!"

"Bloody killer wogs!" His voice cracked and he all but frothed at the mouth his eyes were wide with a madness I had never seen in him even in the heat of battle. "Taunting us with their damn pagan monsters!"

"Stop it!" Horne repeated. He gave up trying to pull George off and stepped back to launch a punch that cracked our friend hard across the jaw. Manderson's head spun around and he dropped, bonelessly, to the ground.

The rest of the café had risen to their feet by this time and some of them were pouring onto the dance floor to come for Manderson. There was much angry shouting in many languages.

I stooped to attend to the girl but then I realized that the veil had been torn from her face in the struggle. Her features were even more stunning than her body, her cheekbones high and her lips a peach colored perfect bow against her nut-brown skin.

There was no tension or fear in her eyes, in fact, I saw only amusement in them which was brought home when she smiled and whispered to me in Hindi "*Ye sriman sab kuch cukt karenge.*"

I reeled as if a sudden cold hand had slapped me across the face. I knew what the phrase meant. What she said was "The gentleman will pay for everything!"

Chapter Two
The Hand of the Dark Lady

The furor over the incident in the Blue Mongoose was great, but Manderson's family had money and connections which we invoked with the help of several fellow officers who were in the café. None of them wanted to be associated with so distasteful an incident either. Money changed hands with the café owner and Toby, with some fellows, hauled George away to get to a cart.

It was left to me to speak to the dancer before we left.

I met her in a side alcove near the kitchen. Upright she came barely to my shoulder, much smaller than she appeared when she had been dancing.

She had re-veiled herself so that only her coal black eyes burned out at me from beneath her inky hair. She had not spoken to me since her statement on the dance floor and now stood in stony silence before me.

"You must forgive my friend," I pleaded, "He had too much to drink and lost his head."

Her head cocked to one side and regarded me with an inscrutable silence.

"Please, Miss," I said, "He really has never done anything like this; his career."

"His career as yours," she said in a musical voice, "is to keep my country beneath a thumb; to treat my people as beasts of burden." There was no edge to the statement but a casualness to it that again sent a chill up my spine.

"This is my country as well, Miss," I said, "I was born here; I want what is best for it as well."

She gave a small unladylike sound that

might have been a snort. "You have no intention of evil in your heart but your mind is clouded by your British blood." She stared into my eyes with no softness in her glance.

After a time, she added, "I will make no report to the authorities; at least not to those on this plane."

I felt the same chill I had when she told me *"Ye sriman sab kuch cukt karenge,"* before. I could find no words to reply to her dark promise though, so I backed away from her piercing stare and went to help Toby with George.

We took our friend back to my quarters and got him to bed before he even woke from Horne's blow. We poured him into bed and then went to my parlor to pour ourselves a single malt whiskey.

My mind was occupied with the face of the dancer, the after-image of her eyes like swirling pools of tar. I also saw again the old man outside the club. I felt as if I were on the bottom of the ocean with the full weight of the mystery that was my India pressing down on me.

"I don't care what the café owner said," Horne said, "word of this will get out; there were too many eyes. Tongues will wag!"

I shook my head in disbelief. "I've never seen him like that. He was a mad man."

"I've heard him rail against the Thugees before — " Horne drank a second drink and shook his head. "I think we had better get him out of town tomorrow. I have some time I can take, perhaps take him to *Dombivli* I know some friends in the garrison there."

"Yes," I said, " that's a good idea. I will lay about some more rupees and keep my ear to the ground for — "

'No!" Manderson's voice roared out of the bedroom with a tone that proclaimed agony.

The two of us ran to the room to behold our friend in the throws of some sort of seizure. He was writhing and twisting on the bed, his eyes still closed. His limbs seemed to vibrate with the intensity of his pain.

"Grab him so he doesn't swallow his tongue," Horne said.

I cradled George's head in my hands as he writhed and Horne threw himself across him.

"No," Manderson moaned again. "Her eyes! Her eyes!" His own eyes snapped open but he was not seeing either of us or even the room.

I knew at that moment what he was seeing; it was the dancer's eyes. I saw them as well in my mind's eye and suddenly I had a slight understanding of his mad fit at the club. Somehow, she had mesmerized him beyond the simple entrancement she had performed on Horne, the others and I. Somehow, she had wormed her way into his soul and taken hold of it to twist and warp it to her purpose.

I kept shouting his name to try to bring him back to us but I knew even as I did it, I was not getting through. The light in his eyes seemed to dim and then change in color from bright blue to a muddy black.

He began to moan; an unearthly sound came from deep within him from some dark recess that was beyond rational thought. It was an inhuman wailing, as much a bray as a cry of agony that was like nails jammed in our ears. It was a keening sound that went up and down the scale and made my skin crawl.

"In the name of God," Horne gasped, "What is happening to him?"

I had no answer for him beyond my belief we had touched some part of the sinister core of the subcontinent, awakened some atavistic force that was engulfing my friend. My contact with Doctor Argent, whose was Minister Without Portfolio for Occult Affairs for the Crown had alerted me to the dark forces that swirled, even on the protected Isle that was my home. Here in India, the forces unseen were even more powerful.

The air around Manderson seemed charged with energy such as I had felt in the Blue Mongoose, as if a physical storm were about to break all around us. I even felt my eardrums pressured as if I were on some Himalayan peak. An icy chill coursed through my body.

A physical metamorphosis began to occur to Manderson. George's chest began to expand up as if inflated.

At first it looked as if some thing were trying to burrow its way out of his body, as if some creature would burst through his ribcage but it was more horrifying even than that. His ribcage was actually expanding and changing shape. It widened along with his shoulders growing in place to strain at his nightclothes.

He shook his head back and forth with foam coming from his lips as if her were rabid.

His face contorted and began to twist to an expression that was fully bestial. His eyes began to bug out, his face to swell, his nose to broaden.

Horne and I were so horrified by the change that we stepped back wide-eyed to stare at the transforming man on the bed. He was becoming something else, something not human.

Manderson's form continued to distort, his stomach bulging out his legs and arms spamming so much he appeared to be vibrating. His head actually grew larger, his neck lengthening and thickening. His face continued to warp as well, his nose and upper lip actually being pushed forward so that soon he had more muzzle than face. His eyes seemed to slide to the side of his head and at that moment I think we both realized what was happening to him.

The dancer's words screamed in my mind, "to treat my people as beasts of burden."

He was being forced into the form of a beast of burden.

He ripped through all his clothes and his body continued to grow in size as it warped in shape.

"We have to do something to help him," Horne whispered. "We have to get a physician or someone. We can't just stand here."

"What can we do?" I answered. "I can not begin to think that there is anything a western doctor can do for this." I knew only one 'Doctor' who might even begin to understand the Eastern magicks that were at work, and my employer was in London.

As I spoke the words, I knew that there was something I could do, not something the British part of me could deal with but my Indian-touched soul knew what to do.

In a hundred more heartbeats we were not looking at our friend anymore but rather at a hunched semi-human beast, like something out of a primordial nightmare. Except, perhaps for the look of confusion and horror and the knowledge of its own state in the animal's eyes. That terror was entirely human.

"I have to go back to the Blue Mongoose," I said as much to summon my own courage as to inform Toby, "I have to get that dancer to remove the curse she must have put on George."

Chapter Three:
Staring into the Eyes of Destiny

I raced back to the Blue Mongoose as quickly as I could leaving Horne to watch over the transformed Manderson. Our friend had completed his change into a fully atavistic form, a twisted thing that had a bull neck supporting a long triangular head.

He had seemed aware of his circumstances, but so stunned that he was dazed and uncommunicative that he just lay stunned.

"I will lose my mind to be with him," Toby had protested. "Let me go with you."

"One of us has to watch him," I said, "I can speak their language and plead his case."

"Do you think those savages will listen to reason," he said. "You'll have to beat a cure out of her and I want to be there when you do."

"That won't have any affect, Toby," I said. "Let me try it my way first, please. It was Manderson's brutality that began all this."

Still I took my Webley with me, and it was a few hours of dawn and darker than the feeling in the pit of my stomach.

All I knew or thought I knew about the dark arts of orient swirled in my head as I rode to the club. I had heard stories of transformations, miraculous changes of man to beast. Dark legends. I knew that the stories were true, that shape shifters who had dark pacts with evil forces. How that perversion had been set upon George I did not know. Or why. But I would find out.

The Blue Mongoose was still open and receiving patrons when I reached it. I stood outside the door summoning my courage and calming myself before I entered; my barging in like Nelson was not going to help. I had to find a way to make the dancer realize it was better for her as well as Manderson for the spell to be removed.

I handed my reins to a young street boy with a half Rupee promised on my return. I knew that the code of honor of such street boys meant my mount was as secure as if the Horseguards were arrayed around it.

Just as I was about to step forward a familiar voice from the shadows startled me.

"*Sahib* should have heeded the warnings," the old fakir from earlier in the night said. "Now even the god *Khandoba* can not help what the Goddess has set in motion. Now you must bear the burden."

I was suddenly angry and stepped forward intent on striking the man but when I moved into the shadowed space, I found nothing. The alcove was empty!

Khandoba was considered by some as an incarnation of *Shiva* and for the old fakir, phantom or not, to invoke him and say I was beyond all help was chilling.

My calm was gone and I felt a new urgency so I thrust myself against the portal and went down into the club to confront the girl.

The interior was the same smoky, shadowy space though there were only the most diehard and drunk of the patrons left. The band was playing a soft *Koli* folk song; "*Aga Pori Sambhaal Dariyala Tufaan Ayalay Bhari; Gorya wer Basali* ."

The *maitre de'* approached me before he recognized me and then froze in place. "Please, *sahib*," he said in a hushed voice, "Do not bring trouble to my humble establishment again."

I stared him in the eye and all but growled. "Bring me to the girl now and there will be no trouble."

Defiance flashed across his face but his desire for peace overcame it and he led me across the room to a door painted red and black with *Sanskrit* writing across it. I recognized only the words "The goddess calls" in the midst of the lettering.

He knocked and a female voice inside answered sharply. "What? I am tired."

"Open, Aakashi," the *maitre de'* called. "You must open for the *sahib* soldier."

There was a long pause and then the door exploded inward to reveal the dancer dressed in a dark blue robe. She wore her hair in a makeshift turban of a towel and behind her veil I could see she had removed some of her stage make-up. She looked at me with black fire in her eyes.

"The Goddess told you would return," she said with smugness that I found irritating. "But she did not tell me it would be so soon."

The *maitre de'* saw the look between us and decided discretion was his best course and went back to the main room.

"Enter, *sahib*," Aakashi hissed. She backed into the room and went to a dressing table.

I entered, leaving the door open.

"Lift the curse," I said. No point with anything less than a frontal assault. She stared at me for a moment with her coal black eyes swirling challenge. A slight smile touched her eyes and when she spoke it was with derisive humor in her voice.

"I do not control the will of the Goddess," she said. She removed her veil and went back to the process of removing her base make-up. "I merely pray to her for justice and it is granted."

I fought to control my anger and my fear, yes fear, of this dark eyed siren who seemed to be connected to all the evil forces of orient.

"Your friend brought his curse upon him, *sahib*," she said, "take care that you do not follow suit."

I am ashamed of my reaction then but can only use my strained nerves and the horrors I had seen that night as explanation. I charged across the room and made to slap the woman, compelled to act like Manderson might have exactly as I was afraid that Horne might.

I barely stopped myself from striking her. It was her smug attitude and the malignant evil in her eyes that abruptly drove me to the edge of madness.

More the madness was her reaction. Though she shied from my slap and fell off of her chair to the floor she looked at me with her flaming eyes and laughed.

"You hasten your own doom," she said

as she climbed to her feet with a casual smile on her lips and a hungry gleam in her eyes.

Almost at once I felt a cramp in my stomach and I knew she had spelled me as well. I reeled. I felt my chest tighten so that my breath came in ragged gasps.

"Why?" I whispered.

She laughed again and spread her arms to take in the whole club and in turn all that was around us. "Why did your people occupy my country? Why did you tread us down beneath your heel and grind us into the ground? Could it be because you believe your god stronger than our gods?"

"Scotland knows the weight of a conqueror's heel." I said. "But this is my home too."

"Then you should know our ways are not to be mocked!" she spat back. "You are only half a fool for allowing your friends to be the beasts they are so you shall be only half the beast they are."

The cramps took me again, this time my legs spasmed as my thighs began to feel as if they were on fire. I gritted my teeth and spoke to her. "You vixen." I cursed, "I'll stop you!" I tried to get my pistol out but the pain palsied my hand and I could not grip the gun.

The girl doffed her robe and dressed behind a screen as if I were unimportant while I moaned against the wall. Indeed, I was impotent and helpless as she donned her outerwear and walked past me.

"You will see that we are not powerless, sahib," she said as she left, "the races beneath the British boot will rise up and our gods will show you what justice is."

Then I was alone in the room with my pain and the knowledge that I was powerless against forces that I barely understood.

It took supreme effort but I forced myself to straighten up and move out through the club to my mount outside. The boy who held it smiled up at me with a professional pride in his charge. I gave him a coin and forced myself into the saddle.

Somehow, I knew it was vital that I get back to my friends as fast as possible. I put spur to my mount and rode faster than was safe almost colliding several times with food carts or people. Bombay was a town that lived twenty-four hours a day, teaming with life.

I had never been more aware of the smells of the city; a heady mix of dung and sweat and decay, of spices and sweet scents that were the very essence of the orient.

My pain continued as I rode but I put it out of my mind. I had only thoughts for my friends and the horror that had been called upon us. I prayed that I would not be too late to at least save Toby from the fate of George.

I had little hope I could save myself.

Chapter Four:
Into the Depths of Pain

My moans were constant and I could not suppress them as I rode to my quarters. I had a hard time pushing the pain from the center of my universe but my fear for Toby overshadowed even my agony.

I raced up the stairs to my suite with a lightening bolt of pain shooting through my limbs with each step. I moved as fast as the pain would allow, but it was not fast enough.

I heard the howling sounds from the bedroom. There were two voices and I knew before I pushed the door inward what I would find.

The beast that Manderson had become was still dazed, though upright on his massive legs, his thick neck and wide chest barely contained in the room. His massive triangular head spun around to stare at me when I entered. They were more the eyes of a beast than a man but there was still a recognition of horror in his eyes.

It was the figure beyond him that caught my attention. There was a thing there still wearing the remnants of Horne's uniform crouched in the corner crying piteously. It had an almost primate head with long upstanding ears like a jackass, but with features intermediate between man and beast.

I could still see Toby's expression hidden in the haunted eyes of the pitiful creature. His legs were a mockery of human with cloven hooves where his feet had been and his thighs were haunches.

In looking at him I thought of the pain in my own legs and the sudden fear gripped me that I was seeing what I would become.

He tried to speak to me but the mewing sound that came forth was more a subdued whiny. He reached a hoofed arm out to me in supplication.

I crossed the room and I wrapped my arms around my comrade. The two of us sobbed for a time until the pain in my legs made me squirm away from him.

"I'm sorry I wasn't in time, Toby," I said, "That witch Aakashi has done us good, mate."

He made a sound that was part cry and part call to arms.

I felt it. I knew then what I had to do.

"I'll find her, Toby, I swear," I said. "And I'll make her stop this" I rose with all the intention of charging out of the room but my legs would not hold me and I stumbled against a table.

My feet were in such pain that I had trouble standing.

"I have to get to her." I forced myself to walk on my shifting feet to the door and then realized I could not leave my friends. I turned to them to see that Horne had followed me from the bedroom his pleading eyes focused on me. Manderson poked his massive head out of the doorway as well and I know I had to bring them with me.

It took some time but I was able to get the transformed Manderson down the back stairs to the street. We disguised Horne in a long coat and put a blanket on Manderson.

George wasn't happy about Toby bundling him into the back of a cart but I talked to him as if he were a new mount in the ring to calm him. He soon accepted his place as Horne mounted the cart's driver's seat and I remounted my own horse and we headed off though the city again to the Blue Mongoose.

This time the journey seemed to take forever. My pain had stabilized to a constant discomfort and I was able to mostly put it out of my mind. Mostly I concentrated on what I would do to the vixen when I found her.

My thoughts were not pretty and I am not proud of them, but the extremity of my circumstance was … and is my explanation for such appalling imaginings.

If she would not reverse her spell cast on the three of us, I was not sure what I was capable of. Would my rage overcome my reason? Would I be justified?

To some extent she was correct, we had come to her home as conquerors, but had not that been the way of the world for the history of mankind? England was settled by a series of conquerors. Edinburgh, Scotland where I had grown to maturity was itself a conquered city in its time. Every region in India had been conquered and settled by waves of warring nations. We were just the latest.

Had not the gods of India been overshadowed a dozen times over in the millennia by successive pantheons?

As an Anglo-Indian I was torn. But as a victim of a Koli spell, I had no confusion: I would find a way to make her change us back or show her what a beast I could be!

The sun was just warming the eastern horizon when our strange caravan arrived at the Blue Mongoose for my third visit. The door was locked but I had no patience for protocol.

"Kick it in, Georgie!" I called and Manderson turned his large body to the task. He bucked hard and slammed his misshaped feet against the portal, shattering it on the first strike.

I raced down the stairs to confront the *maitre de* that was obviously on his way out of the empty club to end his long night's work.

"Where does Aakashi live?" I wasted no time, shoving my pistol into the man's face. His eyes were wide with fear, but he could see that I was in no mood to be equivocated with.

"At Matunga Road number twenty-five." He gasped. "I swear it is true, *sahib*. Do not hurt me!"

"If you are lying, or if you try to warn her I am coming for her, I will come back here," I said in as cold a voice as I have ever uttered.

I left him shivering at the foot of the stairs and raced to my friends. We rode to the address he had given me. The city was coming fully awake and Horne had to huddle forward with a slouch hat pulled down to conceal his strangely transformed face.

Number twenty-five proved to be a two-story building standing alone with a garden around it. There was a locked gate, but once more Manderson's bulk came in handy.

Horne made a snorting sound and I held a hand out to him. He tottered forward on cloven hooves like some circus clown in an ill-fitting suit. My anger rose again.

"Stay with George," I told him, "I will make her change us back or die trying."

I stormed forward without waiting for him to make a comment but when I got the door to the building I paused.

I had no plan of attack; no reconnaissance of the building or fore knowledge of how many might be within. And how to make her change us back? I could hear my mentor Doctor Argent's voice advising *'caution, Jack, m'lad. The forces of chaos can not face logic and planning."*

Logic be damned!

I kick the door in myself this time and entered screaming at the top of my lungs, "Aakashi! Come down here now you devil!"

The morning sun was just lightening the shadows around me and the air had begun to gain humidity. The light revealed that I stood in a foyer that led to a wide staircase to the second floor. To my right an archway led off to a large room, to my left a narrow corridor faded to darkness.

There was no sound in the house save the cry of a tropical bird my scream had woken. No human sound at all.

"Come down Aakashi," I cried, "Or I will burn this place to the ground!"

"Ever the solution of the Empire," her voice floated down to me from the darkness that lingered at the top of the stairs, "but it will be hard to wear the boots of empire in your coming state, eh, Captain Sahib?"

Chapter Five:
Shiva's Child

The dark eyed dancer descended the stairs in slow motion with a broad smile on her face. I could do nothing, not even raise my revolver to point at her. I wanted to slap the smile off her face, to strike out at her but I was as helpless as a babe, frozen by her voice. I could only hope that Horne would sense my distress and burst into the building and smite her like a biblical avenger.

She glided toward me until she stood barely a meter from me. She raised an arm and crooked a finger at me. I felt a deep compulsion to follow, my traitor muscles forcing my legs to follow her.

The dancer led me across the hall to the large room off to the right which the blue light of morning was painting with shadows. It was a temple room of some sort, with pagan idols sitting in niches along the walls. The floor was tile inlaid with scenes from Vedic mythology.

My boots made clicking sounds as I was puppeteer-ed across the vast space to stand before a statue that was larger than the others in the room. It was *Khandoba* as *Shiva*, the Destroyer.

The figure was the dancing representation of the multi-avatared and contradictory god, who was sometimes half woman. He was sometimes depicted immersed in deep meditation, but this incarnation had him dancing the *Tandava* upon Maya, the demon of ignorance in his manifestation as *Nararaia*, the lord of the dance.

The statue was bronze but in the morning light the exquisite sculpting made it seemed almost alive. The third eye in the center of the god's forehead was a carved jewel and the light made it appear as if it were winking at me.

Beside the dancing God was a statue of *Ekveera*, Goddess of the *Koli* and I had another shock when I looked at the face of the statue; it had the features of Aakashi!

"*Shiva* means 'the One who is eternally pure," the dancer said. "It is he who will help my people cleanse the land of your foreign devils!"

I tried to speak, to protest her vile promises but my throat was constricted and all that escaped me were inarticulate mewlings. This seemed to amuse her for her smile broadened.

Her features, which the night before I had thought alluring and entrancing, I now perceived as demonic and evil at its core. Her eyes though, left me and I followed her glance to a door at the far end of the room that opened to disgorge several turbaned and bearded men.

All had the look of warriors with curved

daggers in their hands. She spoke to them in *Maharashtra* and they all halted, their coal black eyes focused on me like hungry wolves. They slowly re-sheathed their blades but their attitude remained martial and ready for violence.

Aakashi turned to the *Shiva* shrine and began to pray in her native language, swaying like a living flame. Her voice rose and fell with the singsong chant that invoked the dark powers of her god.

Her followers took up the chant with her and soon the room was echoing with the pagan melody. She turned to face me after a time and her face was frightening to behold, her features glowing with an inner madness.

"Now you will see the power of our gods, *sahib*." She used the term for 'master' with a sarcastic tone, cuttingly and with all the power to humiliate she could.

"There is a greater justice who will take revenge on you," I managed to whisper. This made her laugh.

"You British have no concept of justice, Captain," she said. "Behold!" She gestured at me and the cramps in my legs began again.

The pain was greater now and I dropped to my knees unable to stand as my muscles spasmed.

The watching natives all murmured approval of their priestess' spell, enjoying my humiliation and pain. Before them they saw in microcosm the destruction of the 'evil' Empire.

My body was no longer mine. The dancer and her evil god had invaded it and taken control of it.

I felt abruptly on fire, my skin tingling. Sweat poured off me as if it were high noon. I tore at the remnants of my tunic and shirt. I felt a beast; or at least half a beast. I knew without looking that my legs had followed the transformation of my feet. Her word of promise had been fulfilled; I was a beast of burden!

The demon woman was transforming me like my fellows into a form that would humiliate me. I knew she wanted to destroy my spirit as well as my body but I would not allow that.

I raised my head to stare into her dead black eyes and defiantly spat, "God will punish you!"

Again, she laughed at my defiance. "*Akim!*" She called and one of the bearded toughs stepped forward with a leather harness that he slipped over my head. There was a bit that he forced in my mouth. I tried to fight him but two other men held my arms so that he could buckle the tack on me.

The man pulled the long reins from the head cap and handed them to Aakashi. She took them and gave a child-like giggle. "Now you will serve a real purpose in the world!" she said.

She snapped the long reins to strike me in the right haunch like a whip. I lurched forward at the assault and she fell into form behind me, forcing me to parade the full circuit of the room.

The watching adherents to the evil cult applauded and hooted as I was made to march around the room, my boots clattering on the floor like hooves. I could not fight her silent commands.

Aakashi stepped behind me holding 'my' reins. "Move, beast!" she ordered. My body that was now hers obeyed and I once more circled the room ahead of her. The men cheered as the symbol of their oppression was himself oppressed.

My spirits fell and I thought at that moment that my life would be only hell from that moment on. I could not even envision any hope of escape from that hellish existence but I had not accounted for the other two inseparables.

Suddenly the door at the end of the room exploded inward and the transformed Manderson charged!

Epilogue
To Live in Hope

My captors were startled by the abrupt appearance of the grossly misshapen Manderson. He pressed his advantage in that surprise by charging across the room straight at the group of bearded men. They attempted to scatter but he slammed into them and sent several of them flying like broken toys.

Horne came racing after him and made straight for me, his hooves clattering across the floor. Behind me I could hear Aakashi as she gasped in shock.

I could also feel her control of me slip as she was startled and I used that moment to turn in my harness. I snatched the reins from her that upset her balance so that she fell.

I undid the buckles of the harness and pulled myself free while Manderson continued to work his rage out on the group of guards.

Horne came to my side and I could see the shocked look in his eyes as he surveyed my condition.

"Good show, Toby," I said putting a hand on his shoulder. "We're in this all together as it should be; now we'll make the witch turn you back!"

We turned our attention then to Aakashi but she had regained her footing and moved toward the door.

"No you don't, vixen!" I yelled at her, "Return them as they were!"

Her pretty face twisted to a snarl. "You will suffer for this indignity of invading our sanctuary!" She rose to her full height in a gesture that I now knew was to summon some evil spell.

Before she could utter a syllable, however, Manderson's bestial form rocketed across the room and smashed into her, his great bulk crushing her beneath him.

"No, George!" I cried but too late. The dancer was mashed to pulp under the flailing giant before I could reach him to stop the attack.

"How will she reverse the spell now?" I said in despair. The snorting Manderson was not to be reasoned with, however and it was several minutes before I and Horne could pull him away. By then it was clear that she was dead.

The very act, as extreme as it was, was the solution to our plight, for Manderson began to revert to his former self almost the moment he was free of contact with her corpse, as did Horne.

Both of my friends vibrated in a new agony and then dropped unconscious at my feet, their forms fully human but looking much worse for the wear, their tattered clothes mere rags.

I stood stunned for a moment unable comprehend what had occurred. There was

(Continued on page 130)

GREAT CAESAR'S GHOST

By JACK HALLIDAY

"Great Caesar's Ghost!" he shouted.

Clark Kent responded with one of his usual witty rejoinders.

"Great Caesar's Ghost!" Perry White continued, "Am I the only one around here who has to work for a living? Go on, get out of here and get me that story!"

I couldn't help but laugh at the all too familiar banter between the editor of *The Daily Planet* and his ace reporter who was also, in actuality, the world's superhuman savior.

I'd been watching reruns as a way to pass the time while I waited for the phone to ring, an email to arrive, or a snail mail letter to find its way to my mailbox. Something, from someone, from somewhere, from anywhere, offering me anything in the way of a substantial means of earning a living.

Apparently, the universe hadn't gotten the memo.

And so, I continued to wait, to "do the work" and try with all of the motivation I could muster to find my way out of the labyrinth of rejection I lived with. *Superman* reruns were one coping method I could afford. The divorce and subsequent settlement — heavily favoring my ex-wife — had left me only this "vacation house," as we so charitably referred to the two-room cabin inherited from my uncle, and the one pittance of savings I had kept solely in my name.

I turned my attention away from the set

and looked out the living room window, past the line of trees that formed a natural boundary between my property and the one owned by the retired couple I had seen once or twice at the local restaurant. They might as well have lived on Mars.

The way they explained things to me on one wintry morning when we introduced ourselves over steaming cups of coffee, was that their rather large domicile sat several acres up, up and away from the southernmost border of their land. In other words, under normal circumstances, we would never see each other — accidentally or otherwise.

Not that I minded terribly.

The divorce had "taken me out," emotionally, and I really wasn't all that fond of the idea of any personal interaction with anyone, regardless of their station in life. I just wanted to be left alone. But even that required money, something of which I was in short supply.

While I was musing along these lines, I saw something out of the corner of my eye. It was just the tiniest, briefest wisp of something or other. For some reason, my body registered its awareness of the "something" with an immediate tingling sensation in my groin. This unpleasant feeling soon became a duet with a matching prickly feeling in my, now, slightly perspiring palms.

Was this going to become a full-blown panic attack? A sense of foreboding joined the symphony and I turned very slowly in the direction of what appeared to be the shadow of a large male figure standing just behind the arm chair, next to the end table on which the phone rested.

I literally squeezed my eyes shut and when I opened them, the entire episode had evaporated into the ether. It was exactly the kind of experience for which an overindulgence in vodka was responsible.

But I hadn't been drinking.

Very slowly and deliberately, I rose from the couch and tiptoed over to the table. There was the faint aroma of something akin to musk or another sort of esoteric essential oil. I'm a million miles away from being an expert on "natural living" but I can recognize the aroma of sandalwood or something similar. In a few moments, even the olfactory evidence of this strange but seemingly innocuous encounter dissipated along with the effects of my sympathetic nervous system.

The divorce had really done a number on me, all right. If memory served, it ranked pretty high up on the scale of "life-stressing situations" according to the experts who studied such subjects.

I had just about decided to brush the entire brief and bizarre experience away as an odd happenstance when I noticed something by the ash tray on the table beside the sofa. I'm not much of a housekeeper by any stretch of the imagination, but I knew that nothing had been rearranged in the last little while. Yet there was definitely something there.

I padded my way over to the end table and plopped down on the couch. Sure enough, there, right in front of my bloodshot eyes, lay a leaf of some kind. It was gray-green and curled somewhat; but as I looked closer, I noticed that it was alive, or at least not too long deceased.

Under normal circumstances, I would

never even have noticed such a small and inconspicuous addition to my surroundings. However, living and being so starkly alone for such an extended period of time had caused me to be a little OCD about things, even little things, like a lone sock beside the bed or a knife or fork out of place in a kitchen drawer. And gardening? My version of the proverbial "green thumb" is ten pale digits dooming any living plant species to an early and, no doubt, disastrous demise! My wife wouldn't even allow me to water them, let alone plant or tend them.

As I held the frail item, I noticed again the odd fragrance of some long-lost vapor from yesteryear. How did it get into my living room? From where had it come? What, if any, meaning or message was it attempting to convey? Yes, a "message," since it seemed to me to be an attempt at an inarticulate conversation.

"Great Caesar's Ghost!" shouted Perry again, jerking my attention away from the remnant of plant life between my fingers. I smiled and rose quickly to turn off the television. I stood there, in the center of the room, rolling the small leaf's stem between my thumb and index finger, pondering my next move.

Suddenly, it dawned on me that a simple solution presented itself, and quite a pleasant one at that. Although I had not made a great number of friends in the brief time I'd been here, I had struck up a minor acquaintance with the local proprietress of "All About Flowers" in the center of town. Since the store was situated two doors from a coffee shop, we had begun a random routine of meeting there to talk about nothing in particular whenever I made the short trip from my inherited hideaway.

I was in my car in no time and felt a strange but welcome sense of perhaps a distant, emotional relative of hope, as I drove the familiar route to town. I took a deep breath of fresh air and admired the large rock-laden hills to my right. They reminded me of another similar area of terrain from my youth, and as I drove past, I soon found myself mentally transported to the neighborhood in which I had spent my adolescence.

One Saturday morning in particular pushed its way into the front of my mind. Two buddies and I had decided to ride and push our bicycles all the way from "the old man's driveway" to the very summit of the long and winding hill that rose to meet the highway situated very high and over a mile away off in the distance. We had planned our return ride very carefully, deciding upon an exact number to count before each of us, in single file, launched ourselves from the entrance to the narrow, bike-worn pathway. The long, fast and decidedly treacherous ride all the way down to the gravel driveway below, promised enough excitement to last the remainder of the summer!

One by one we mounted our trusty bikes and set off on what promised to be the ride of a lifetime. All seemed to be going according to plan and I counted dutifully before jumping on my trusty metal companion. The ride down was at once, a hundred times more exciting, as well as far more terrifying than I had imagined, and the surrounding trees whisked by my wide-eyed view, appearing to almost lean toward me as though they were trying to gain a closer look at my upcoming peril.

It seemed like a long distance at the time, but it was probably no more than a quarter mile away when I saw my friend, Pat, in the distance, waving a warning at me. Even with the incredible speed I had picked up, I could clearly see Dave's mangled bike by the fence in the distance and he was also waving a blood-stained arm. The only way to avoid yet another collision was for me to slam on the brakes while simultaneously jerking my bicycle to the side, veering toward the fence owned by the farmer who was blissfully unaware of our attempt at adolescent adventure.

Time stood still as my bike left the deep, dark earth of the trail, just before the narrow path morphed into a man-made gravel driveway. I seemed to be suspended in space for a moment before I watched the earth "rise up" to greet me as I avoided Dave, and crash-landed in a small gully adjoining the driveway. He and I could have been twin survivors were it not for an additional cut I sported on my forehead.

At that moment, I remembered the strange musky smell as I lay there on the damp ground, looking at a faint, gray-green leaf directly in front of my tear-filled, teen-aged eyes.

A shot of adrenaline suddenly raced through my body, bringing me back to the present, and I was relieved to see the familiar town in front of me, causing the childhood memory and its effect upon me to dissipate.

What on earth did this mean? Why did the memory of a childhood incident somehow surface now? And then I remembered it was my uncle whom I had called to pick me up and drive me home that fateful day. The same uncle who had bequeathed to me the cabin I was currently calling home.

***

I was extremely happy Marie was just about to take a break from her flower shop when I arrived. The familiar aroma of various species of flowers greeted me, along with a genuine smile from her. She slipped out of her work smock and donned a burnt orange-colored sweater that didn't do her figure any harm.

"I was just thinking about you" she said, as she slipped her arm around my elbow. The bells atop the door jingled "goodbye" as I closed it behind us. I took another deep breath of the spring air and watched my well-worn loafers make their way to the coffee shop two doors away.

"I'd say, 'a penny for your thoughts,' but I still have to pay for our drinks," I mumbled.

She waved a hand at me as I held the door open for her.

"Oh, you; something will open up for you, and soon. I have a feeling."

"Do tell," I said, as I followed her into the small eatery which was just beginning to fill up with an early lunch crowd.

"You'll find something," she replied, as though she really believed it.

I suddenly found it very comforting to be sitting across from a forty-something woman sipping a frothy latte, who could have easily passed for *Stella Stevens* in that beautiful actress's prime. This widow's genuineness stood in stark contrast to the unabashed selfishness of my former wife.

"You've got one little spot of whipped

cream on the very center of your perfect nose."

Her eyes widened and the corners of her lips curled up in an impish smile as she dabbed her nose with her napkin.

"What would I do without you to look after me?" she said, and then she leaned back in her seat as her smile faded.

"Jack, I'm really serious. Just because you were the victim of the proverbial 'corporate downsizing' doesn't disqualify you for a good job at a good wage in comfortable surroundings. Something fantastic is coming for you; something beyond your wildest dreams."

"From your lips to God's ear," I replied, taking a long pull from my cafe mocha.

"Speaking of something coming my way," I continued, "would you mind looking at something for me? I'd really appreciate your take on it."

"Not at all; what do you have in mind?"

I chose my next words very carefully.

"I, ah, noticed a small leaf in the house — don't know how it got there — and I was curious about what it might be, you know, plant-wise. I figured you'd be the 'go to' person to ask."

She leaned forward, resting her dimpled chin on one palm.

"Let's have a look; did you bring it with you?"

"I did" I responded, as I whisked the small leaf from my jacket pocket.

She held it by the stem rolling it back and forth between her long fore-finger and thumb. I noticed that she had recently had her nails done, 'French style,' and it was a good touch.

She leaned back, placing the leaf on a napkin.

"Well, let's have it; I don't want to die of suspense over a cup of coffee."

"At least you gave me an easy one," she said. "It's a type of olive leaf, *lauris nobilis*, the variety that's native to the Middle East. I don't see many of them in my line of work."

I picked it up, glanced at it and put it back in my pocket.

"So, you're saying it wouldn't be a very natural occurrence to find one of these at home?"

Her eyebrows furrowed.

"You found this where?" she asked.

"In the house: my house, on the end table, right next to the couch. According to your expertise, a portion of a plant has moved from the Middle East to my house."

"You're joking."

"I'm not."

"Jack, this is really an anomaly; you get that, right?"

"I'm beginning to. I'm just wondering how and why."

"And I'd say you have a right to wonder. As a matter of fact, I'd say you have an absolute right to be doing a whole lot of wondering. This is really quite something."

I smiled. "And so are you."

She returned the smile.

***

The drive home was extremely pleasant. Not only had I found the answer to my question regarding the olive leaf, but I had also enjoyed a nice hour of conversation

with a woman who, I realized, was quite attractive and apparently bereft of any hidden agendas. She absolutely was just what she appeared to be: a very attractive, middle-aged widow, looking for a relatively nice and normal guy with whom to embark on a new relationship. I decided to do my best to make that happen.

It was just beginning to drop dark when I again stood at my front door. I had picked up some much-needed grocery items while I was downtown and had also made a very informative stop at the local library. I had perused a few volumes and discovered, among other things, that olive leaves were the apparent flora of choice "back in the day." And I mean, way, way, "back in the day." Among other things, they were used to make the "laurel wreaths" used as victor's crowns in the ancient Olympics, as well as the crowns of Greek and Roman leaders.

After I put up the groceries, I decided to slip into my pajamas early and just vegetate in front of the tube for a bit before heading off to dreamland.

As I entered the living room from my very small bedroom, I thought I noticed someone standing near the door to the cellar. Instinctively, I froze in place and then slowly back-pedaled a few steps into the doorway where I watched and waited for the intruder to make himself known.

Again, the faint aroma of musk filled my nostrils as I watched what appeared to be a tall, shadowy figure carrying what looked for all the world like a long, double-edged, broadsword in one hand. It was as though he was composed of a shadowy substance that allowed only an outline of his body to be visible. In a moment, he simply passed "through" the closed and locked front door. It was then that I realized I had been holding my breath, and out it came with a whoosh! I ran to the door, looked through the window and saw exactly what I expected: nothing.

There was absolutely no sign of anyone, anywhere near the premises.

As I stepped back from the door, for some unknown reason, I looked down at the floor by my feet, perhaps in a futile desire to discover foreign, muddy footprints. Instead I saw, not footprints, but olive leaves, dozens of them, forming a trail from the cellar door at the other end of the room. I followed them to the door, opened it, turned on the light and saw before me a continuing, orderly trail of leaves leading down the rickety stairs to one corner

---

Jack Halliday is an author, award-winning screenwriter, and producer, whose work has appeared in numerous digital and print publications. His first mystery collection, *Kwanga/Swan Song and Other Mystery Stories*, was published by Wildside Press as their 12th "Mystery Double." His noir, mystery novel, *The Big Bluff*, debuted from Solstice Publishing in 2018. He lives in the Midwest with his wife and son.

of the ground floor.

When I say, "ground floor," I mean it, literally. It wasn't actually a floor at all, but, rather, a hodge-podge of stones, gravel and for the most part, plain old, "made in the USA" dirt. It was not at all unlike the floor of the entire house of a family I once visited on the island of Crete. Apparently, they thought the "natural look" worked just fine for them, especially in their climate. I had no idea what my uncle had in mind when he left this one unfinished. The trail of olive leaves led to a mass piled up in the corner.

What on earth (no pun intended) was going on here?

***

I was upstairs and on my computer in record time. I suddenly had the same kind of energy that used to fuel my deal-making back in the day. In my previous career, once I caught the scent of some real cash, I became an outwardly mild-mannered, and inwardly, white-collar predator, closing any and all such deals at any cost. That's the kind of inner drive I found pumping through my system now. It was as though some weird and wonderful mystery was about to be solved and I was Sherlock Holmes!

I used a search engine for information about olive wreaths, ancient Greece and ancient Rome.

I followed the various links.

And then I saw it — one website that contained information about ancient Roman

(Continued on page 134)

H. P. LOVECRAFT

The Colour Out of Space

Had Death descended from the stars?

WEST of Arkham the hills rise wild, and there are valleys with deep woods that no axe has ever cut. There are dark narrow glens where the trees slope fantastically, and where thin brooklets trickle without ever having caught the glint of sunlight. On the gentler slopes there are farms, ancient and rocky, with squat, moss-coated cottages brooding eternally over old New England secrets in the lee of great ledges; but these are all vacant now, the wide chimneys crumbling and the shingled sides bulging perilously beneath low gambrel roofs.

The old folk have gone away, and foreigners do not like to live there. French-Canadians have tried it, Italians have tried it, and the Poles have come and departed. It is not because of anything that can be seen or heard or handled, but because of something that is imagined. The place is not good for the imagination, and does not bring restful dreams at night. It must be this which keeps the foreigners away, for old Ammi Pierce has never told them of anything he recalls from the strange days. Ammi, whose head has been a little queer for years, is the only one who still remains, or whoever talks of the strange days; and he dares to do this because his house is so near the open fields and the travelled roads around Arkham.

There was once a road over the hills and through the valleys, that ran straight where the blasted heath is now; but people ceased to use it and a new road was laid curving far toward the south. Traces of the old one can still be found amidst the weeds of a returning wilderness, and some of them will doubtless linger even when half the hollows are flooded for the new reservoir. Then the dark woods will be cut down and the blasted heath will slumber far below blue waters whose surface will mirror the sky and ripple in the sun. And the secrets of the strange days will be one with the deep's secrets; one with the hidden lore of old ocean, and all the mystery of primal earth.

When I went into the hills and vales to survey for the new reservoir, they told me the place was evil. They told me this in Arkham, and because that is a very old town full of witch legends, I thought the evil must be something which grandams had whispered to children through centuries. The name "blasted heath" seemed to me very odd and theatrical, and I wondered how it had come into the folklore of a Puritan people. Then I saw that dark westward tangle of glens and slopes for myself, and ceased to wonder at anything besides its own elder mystery. It was morning when I saw it, but shadow lurked always there. The trees grew too thickly, and their trunks were too big for any healthy New England wood. There was too much silence in the dim alleys between them, and the floor was too soft with the dank moss and mattings of infinite years of decay.

In the open spaces, mostly along the line of the old road, there were little hillside farms; sometimes with all the buildings standing, sometimes with only one or two, and sometimes with only a lone chimney or fast-filling cellar. Weeds and briers reigned, and furtive wild things rustled in the undergrowth. Upon everything was a haze of restlessness and oppression; a touch of the unreal and the grotesque, as if some vital element of perspective or chiaroscuro were awry. I did not wonder that the foreigners would not stay, for this was no region to sleep in. It was too much like a landscape of Salvator Rosa; too much like some forbidden woodcut in a tale of terror.

BUT even all this was not so bad as the blasted heath. I knew it the moment I came upon it at the bottom of a spacious valley; for no other name could fit such a thing, or any other thing fit such a name. It was as if the poet had coined the phrase from having seen this one particular region. It must, I thought as I viewed it, be the outcome of a fire; but why had nothing new ever grown over those five acres of grey desolation that sprawled open to the sky like a great spot eaten by acid in the woods and fields? It lay largely to the north of the ancient road line, but encroached a little on the other side. I felt an odd reluctance about approaching, and did so at last only because my business took me through and past it. There was no vegetation of any kind on that broad expanse, but only a fine grey dust or ash which no wind seemed ever to blow about. The trees near it were sickly and stunted, and many dead trunks stood or lay rotting at the rim. As I walked hurriedly by I saw the tumbled bricks and stones of an old chimney and cellar on my right, and the yawning black maw of an abandoned well whose stagnant vapours played strange tricks with the hues of the sunlight. Even the long, dark woodland climb beyond seemed welcome in contrast, and I marvelled no more at the frightened whispers of Arkham people. There had been no house or ruin near; even in the old days the place must have been lonely and remote. And at twilight, dreading to repass that ominous spot, I walked circuitously back to the town by the curving road on the south. I vaguely wished some clouds would gather, for an odd timidity about the deep skyey voids above had crept into my soul.

IN the evening I asked old people in Arkham about the blasted heath, and what was meant by that phrase "strange days" which so many evasively muttered. I could not, however, get any good answers, except that all the mystery was much more recent than I had dreamed. It was not a matter of old legendry at all, but something within the lifetime of those who spoke. It had happened in the 'eighties, and a family had disappeared or was killed. Speakers would not be exact; and because they all told me to pay no attention to old Ammi Pierce's crazy tales, I sought him out the next morning, having heard that he lived alone in the ancient tottering cottage where the trees first begin to get very thick. It was a fearsomely archaic place, and had begun to exude the faint miasmal odour which clings about houses that have stood too long. Only with persistent knocking could I rouse the aged man, and when he shuffled timidly to the door I could tell he was not glad to see me. He was not so feeble as I had expected; but his eyes drooped in a curious way, and his unkempt clothing and white beard made him seem very worn and dismal. Not knowing just how he could best be launched on his tales, I feigned a matter of business; told him of my surveying, and asked vague questions about the district. He was far brighter and more educated than I had been led to think, and before I knew it had grasped quite as much of the subject as any man I had talked with in Arkham. He was not like other rustics I had known in the sections where reservoirs were to be. From him there were no protests at the miles of old wood and farmland to be blotted out, though perhaps there would have been had not his home lain outside the bounds of the future lake. Relief was all that he shewed; relief at the doom of the dark ancient valleys through which he had roamed all his life. They were better under water now—better under water since the strange days. And with this opening his husky voice sank low, while his body leaned forward and his right forefinger began to point shakily and impressively.

It was then that I heard the story, and as the rambling voice scraped and whispered on I shivered again and again despite the summer day. Often I had to recall the speaker from ramblings, piece out scientific points which he knew only by a fading parrot memory of professors' talk, or bridge over gaps where his sense of logic and continuity broke down. When he was done I did not wonder that his mind had snapped a trifle, or that the folk of Arkham would not speak much of the blasted heath. I hurried back before sunset to my hotel, unwilling to have the stars come out above me in the open; and the next day returned to Boston to give up my position. I could not go into that dim chaos of old forest and slope again, or face another time that grey blasted heath where the black well yawned deep beside the tumbled bricks and stones.

The reservoir will soon be built now, and all those elder secrets will be safe forever under watery fathoms. But even then I do not believe I would like to visit that country by night—at least, not when the sinister stars are out; and nothing could bribe me to drink the new city water of Arkham.

It all began, old Ammi said, with the meteorite. Before that time there had been no wild legends at all since the witch trials, and even then these western woods were not feared half so much as the small island in the Miskatonic where the devil held court beside a curious stone altar older than the Indians. These were not haunted woods, and their fantastic dusk was never terrible till the strange days. Then there had come that white noontide cloud, that string of explosions in the air, and that pillar of smoke from the valley far in the wood. And by night all Arkham had heard of the great rock that fell out of the sky and bedded itself in the ground beside the well at the Nahum Gardner place. That was the house which had stood where the blasted heath was to come—the trim white Nahum Gardner house amidst its fertile gardens and orchards.

Nahum had come to town to tell people about the stone, and had dropped in at Ammi Pierce's on the way. Ammi was forty then, and all the queer things were fixed very strongly in his mind. He and his wife had gone with the three professors from Miskatonic University who hastened out the next morning to see the weird visitor from unknown stellar space, and had wondered why Nahum had called it so large the day before. It had shrunk, Nahum said as he pointed out the big brownish mound above the ripped earth and charred grass near the archaic well-sweep in his front yard; but the wise men answered that stones do not shrink. Its heat lingered persistently, and Nahum declared it had glowed faintly in the night. The professors tried it with a geologist's hammer and found it was oddly soft. It was, in truth, so soft as to be almost plastic; and they gouged rather than chipped a specimen to take back to the college for testing. They took it in an old pail borrowed from Nahum's kitchen, for even the small piece refused to grow cool. On the trip back they stopped at Ammi's to rest, and seemed thoughtful when Mrs. Pierce remarked that the fragment was growing smaller and burning the bottom of the pail. Truly, it was not large, but perhaps they had taken less than they thought.

The day after that—all this was in June of '82—the professors had trooped out again in a great excitement. As they passed Ammi's they told him what queer things the specimen had done, and how it had faded wholly away when they put it in a glass beaker. The beaker had gone, too, and the wise men talked of the strange stone's affinity for silicon. It had acted quite unbelievably in that well-ordered laboratory; doing nothing at all and shewing no occluded gases when heated on charcoal, being wholly negative in the borax bead, and soon proving itself absolutely non-volatile at any producible temperature, including that of the oxy-hydrogen blowpipe. On an anvil it appeared highly malleable, and in the dark its luminosity was very marked. Stubbornly refusing to grow cool, it soon had the college in a state of real excitement; and when upon heating before the spectroscope it displayed shining bands unlike any known colours of the normal spectrum there was much breathless talk of new elements, bizarre optical properties, and other things which puzzled men of science are wont to say when faced by the unknown.

HOT as it was, they tested it in a crucible with all the proper reagents. Water did nothing. Hydrochloric acid was the same. Nitric acid and even aqua regia merely hissed and spattered against its torrid invulnerability. Ammi had difficulty in recalling all these things, but recognised some solvents as I mentioned them in the usual order of use. There were ammonia and caustic soda, alcohol and ether, nauseous carbon disulphide and a dozen others; but although the weight grew steadily less as time passed, and the fragment seemed to be slightly cooling, there was no change in the solvents to shew that they had attacked the substance at all. It was a metal, though, beyond a doubt. It was magnetic, for one thing; and after its immersion in the acid solvents there seemed to be faint traces of the Widmannstätten figures found on meteoric iron. When the cooling had grown very considerable, the testing was carried on in glass; and it was in a glass beaker that they left all the chips made of the original fragment during the work. The next morning both chips and beaker were gone without trace, and only a charred spot marked the place on the wooden shelf where they had been.

All this the professors told Ammi as they paused at his door, and once more he went with them to see the stony messenger from the stars, though this time his wife did not accompany him. It had now most certainly shrunk, and even the sober professors could not doubt the truth of what they saw. All around the dwindling brown lump near the well was a vacant space, except where the earth had caved in; and whereas it had been a good seven feet across the day before, it was now scarcely five. It was still hot, and the sages studied its surface curiously as they detached another and larger piece with hammer and chisel. They gouged deeply this time, and as they pried away the smaller mass they saw that the core of the thing was not quite homogeneous.

They had uncovered what seemed to be the side of a large coloured globule imbedded in the substance. The colour, which resembled some of the bands in the meteor's strange spectrum, was almost impossible to describe; and it was only by analogy that they called it colour at all. Its texture was glossy, and upon tapping it appeared to promise both brittleness and hollowness. One of the professors gave it a smart blow with a hammer, and it burst with a nervous little pop. Nothing was emitted, and all trace of the thing vanished with the puncturing. It left behind a hollow spherical space about three inches across, and all thought it probable that others would be discovered as the enclosing substance wasted away.

CONJECTURE was vain; so after a futile attempt to find additional globules by drilling, the seekers left again with their new specimen—which proved, however, as baffling in the laboratory as its

Art: Frank R. Paul
Originally presented in
Amazing Stories, Sep. 1927.
Experimenter Publishing Co., Inc.

predecessor had been. Aside from being almost plastic, having heat, magnetism, and slight luminosity, cooling slightly in powerful acids, possessing an unknown spectrum, wasting away in air, and attacking silicon compounds with mutual destruction as a result, it presented no identifying features whatsoever; and at the end of the tests the college scientists were forced to own that they could not place it. It was nothing of this earth, but a piece of the great outside; and as such dowered with outside properties and obedient to outside laws.

That night there was a thunderstorm, and when the professors went out to Nahum's the next day they met with a bitter disappointment. The stone, magnetic as it had been, must have had some peculiar electrical property; for it had "drawn the lightning", as Nahum said, with a singular persistence. Six times within an hour the farmer saw the lightning strike the furrow in the front yard, and when the storm was over nothing remained but a ragged pit by the ancient well-sweep, half-choked with caved-in earth. Digging had borne no fruit, and the scientists verified the fact of the utter vanishment. The failure was total; so that nothing was left to do but go back to the laboratory and test again the disappearing fragment left carefully cased in lead. That fragment lasted a week, at the end of which nothing of value had been learned of it. When it had gone, no residue was left behind, and in time the professors felt scarcely sure they had indeed seen with waking eyes that cryptic vestige of the fathomless gulfs outside; that lone, weird message from other universes and other realms of matter, force, and entity.

As was natural, the Arkham papers made much of the incident with its collegiate sponsoring, and sent reporters to talk with Nahum Gardner and his family. At least one Boston daily also sent a scribe, and Nahum quickly became a kind of local celebrity. He was a lean, genial person of about fifty, living with his wife and three sons on the pleasant farmstead in the valley. He and Ammi exchanged visits frequently, as did their wives; and Ammi had nothing but praise for him after all these years. He seemed slightly proud of the notice his place had attracted, and talked often of the meteorite in the succeeding weeks. That

July and August were hot, and Nahum worked hard at his haying in the ten-acre pasture across Chapman's Brook; his rattling wain wearing deep ruts in the shadowy lanes between. The labour tired him more than it had in other years, and he felt that age was beginning to tell on him.

Then fell the time of fruit and harvest. The pears and apples slowly ripened, and Nahum vowed that his orchards were prospering as never before. The fruit was growing to phenomenal size and unwonted gloss, and in such abundance that extra barrels were ordered to handle the future crop. But with the ripening came sore disappointment; for of all that gorgeous array of specious lusciousness not one single jot was fit to eat. Into the fine flavour of the pears and apples had crept a stealthy bitterness and sickishness, so that even the smallest of bites induced a lasting disgust. It was the same with the melons and tomatoes, and Nahum sadly saw that his entire crop was lost. Quick to connect events, he declared that the meteorite had poisoned the soil, and thanked heaven that most of the other crops were in the upland lot along the road.

WINTER came early, and was very cold. Ammi saw Nahum less often than usual, and observed that he had begun to look worried. The rest of his family, too, seemed to have grown taciturn; and were far from steady in their churchgoing or their attendance at the various social events of the countryside. For this reserve or melancholy no cause could be found, though all the household confessed now and then to poorer health and a feeling of vague disquiet. Nahum himself gave the most definite statement of anyone when he said he was disturbed about certain footprints in the snow. They were the usual winter prints of red squirrels, white rabbits, and foxes, but the brooding farmer professed to see something not quite right about their nature and arrangement. He was never specific, but appeared to think that they were not as characteristic of the anatomy and habits of squirrels and rabbits and foxes as they ought to be. Ammi listened without interest to this talk until one night when he drove past Nahum's house in his sleigh on the way back from Clark's Corners. There had been a moon, and a rabbit had run across the road, and the leaps of that rabbit were longer than either Ammi or his horse liked. The latter, indeed, had almost run away when brought up by a firm rein. Thereafter Ammi gave Nahum's tales more respect, and wondered why the Gardner dogs seemed so cowed and quivering every morning. They had, it developed, nearly lost the spirit to bark.

In February the McGregor boys from Meadow Hill were out shooting woodchucks, and not far from the Gardner place bagged a very peculiar specimen. The proportions of its body seemed slightly altered in a queer way impossible to describe, while its face had taken on an expression which no one ever saw in a woodchuck before. The boys were genuinely frightened, and threw the thing away at once, so that only their grotesque tales of it ever reached the people of the countryside. But the shying of the horses near Nahum's house had now become an acknowledged thing, and all the basis for a cycle of whispered legend was fast taking form.

People vowed that the snow melted faster around Nahum's than it did anywhere else, and early in March there was an awed discussion in Potter's general store at Clark's Corners. Stephen Rice had driven past Gardner's in the morning, and had noticed the skunk-cabbages coming up through the mud by the woods across the road. Never were things of such size seen before, and they held strange colours that could not be put into any words. Their shapes were monstrous, and the horse had snorted at an odour which struck Stephen as wholly unprecedented. That afternoon several persons drove past to see the abnormal growth, and all agreed that plants of that kind ought never to sprout in a healthy world. The bad fruit of the fall before was freely mentioned, and it went from mouth to mouth that there was poison in Nahum's ground. Of course it was the meteorite; and remembering how strange the men from the college had found that stone to be, several farmers spoke about the matter to them.

ONE day they paid Nahum a visit; but having no love of wild tales and folklore were very conservative in what they inferred. The plants were certainly odd, but all skunk-cabbages are more or less odd in shape and odour and hue. Perhaps some mineral element from the stone had entered the soil, but it would soon be washed away. And as for the footprints and frightened horses—of course this was mere country talk which such a phenomenon as the aërolite would be certain to start. There was really nothing for serious men to do in cases of wild gossip, for superstitious rustics will say and believe anything. And so all through the strange days the professors stayed away in contempt. Only one of them, when given two phials of dust for analysis in a police job over a year and a half later, recalled that the queer colour of that skunk-cabbage had been very like one of the anomalous bands of light shewn by the meteor fragment in the college spectroscope, and like the brittle globule found imbedded in the stone from the abyss. The samples in this analysis case gave the same odd bands at first, though later they lost the property.

The trees budded prematurely around Nahum's, and at night they swayed ominously in the wind. Nahum's second son Thaddeus, a lad of fifteen, swore that they swayed also when there was no wind; but even the gossips would not credit this. Certainly, however, restlessness was in the air. The entire Gardner family developed the habit of stealthy listening, though not for any sound which they could consciously name. The listening was, indeed, rather a product of moments when consciousness seemed half to slip away. Unfortunately, such moments increased week by week, till it became common speech that "something was wrong with all Nahum's folks". When the early saxifrage came out it had another strange colour; not quite like that of the skunk-cabbage, but plainly related and equally unknown to anyone who saw it. Nahum took some blossoms to Arkham and shewed them to the editor of the Gazette, but that dignitary did no more than write a humorous article about them, in which the dark fears of rustics were held up to polite ridicule. It was a mistake of

Nahum's to tell a stolid city man about the way the great, overgrown mourning-cloak butterflies behaved in connexion with these saxifrages.

April brought a kind of madness to the country folk, and began that disuse of the road past Nahum's which led to its ultimate abandonment. It was the vegetation. All the orchard trees blossomed forth in strange colours, and through the stony soil of the yard and adjacent pasturage there sprang up a bizarre growth which only a botanist could connect with the proper flora of the region. No sane wholesome colours were anywhere to be seen except in the green grass and leafage; but everywhere those hectic and prismatic variants of some diseased, underlying primary tone without a place among the known tints of earth. The Dutchman's breeches became a thing of sinister menace, and the bloodroots grew insolent in their chromatic perversion. Ammi and the Gardners thought that most of the colours had a sort of haunting familiarity, and decided that they reminded one of the brittle globule in the meteor. Nahum ploughed and sowed the ten-acre pasture and the upland lot, but did nothing with the land around the house. He knew it would be of no use, and hoped that the summer's strange growths would draw all the poison from the soil. He was prepared for almost anything now, and had grown used to the sense of something near him waiting to be heard. The shunning of his house by neighbours told on him, of course; but it told on his wife more. The boys were better off, being at school each day; but they could not help being frightened by the gossip. Thaddeus, an especially sensitive youth, suffered the most.

In May the insects came, and Nahum's place became a nightmare of buzzing and crawling. Most of the creatures seemed not quite usual in their aspects and motions, and their nocturnal habits contradicted all former experience. The Gardners took to watching at night—watching in all directions at random for something ... they could not tell what. It was then that they all owned that Thaddeus had been right about the trees. Mrs. Gardner was the next to see it from the window as she watched the swollen boughs of a maple against a moonlit sky. The boughs surely moved, and there was no wind. It must be the sap. Strangeness had come into everything growing now. Yet it was none of Nahum's family at all who made the next discovery. Familiarity had dulled them, and what they could not see was glimpsed by a timid windmill salesman from Bolton who drove by one night in ignorance of the country legends. What he told in Arkham was given a short paragraph in the Gazette; and it was there that all the farmers, Nahum included, saw it first. The night had been dark and the buggy-lamps faint, but around a farm in the valley which everyone knew from the account must be Nahum's the darkness had been less thick. A dim though distinct luminosity seemed to inhere in all the vegetation, grass, leaves, and blossoms alike, while at one moment a detached piece of the phosphorescence appeared to stir furtively in the yard near the barn.

THE grass had so far seemed untouched, and the cows were freely pastured in the lot near the house, but toward the end of May the milk began to be bad. Then Nahum had the cows driven to the uplands, after which the trouble ceased. Not long after this the change in grass and leaves became apparent to the eye. All the verdure was going grey, and was developing a highly singular quality of brittleness. Ammi was now the only person who ever visited the place, and his visits were becoming fewer and fewer. When school closed the Gardners were virtually cut off from the world, and sometimes let Ammi do their errands in town. They were failing curiously both physically and mentally, and no one was surprised when the news of Mrs. Gardner's madness stole around.

It happened in June, about the anniversary of the meteor's fall, and the poor woman screamed about things in the air which she could not describe. In her raving there was not a single specific noun, but only verbs and pronouns. Things moved and changed and fluttered, and ears tingled to impulses which were not wholly sounds. Something was taken away—she was being drained of something—something was fastening itself on her that ought not to be—someone must make it keep off—nothing was ever still in the night—the walls and windows shifted. Nahum did not send her to the county asylum, but let her wander about the house as long as she was harmless to herself and others. Even when her expression changed he did nothing. But when the boys grew afraid of her, and Thaddeus nearly fainted at the way she made faces at him, he decided to keep her locked in the attic. By July she had ceased to speak and crawled on all fours, and before that month was over Nahum got the mad notion that she was slightly luminous in the dark, as he now clearly saw was the case with the nearby vegetation.

It was a little before this that the horses had stampeded. Something had aroused them in the night, and their neighing and kicking in their stalls had been terrible. There seemed virtually nothing to do to calm them, and when Nahum opened the stable door they all bolted out like frightened woodland deer. It took a week to track all four, and when found they were seen to be quite useless and unmanageable. Something had snapped in their brains, and each one had to be shot for its own good. Nahum borrowed a horse from Ammi for his haying, but found it would not approach the barn. It shied, balked, and whinnied, and in the end he could do nothing but drive it into the yard while the men used their own strength to get the heavy wagon near enough the hayloft for convenient pitching. And all the while the vegetation was turning grey and brittle. Even the flowers whose hues had been so strange were greying now, and the fruit was coming out grey and dwarfed and tasteless. The asters and goldenrod bloomed grey and distorted, and the roses and zinneas and hollyhocks in the front yard were such blasphemous-looking things that Nahum's oldest boy Zenas cut them down. The strangely puffed insects died about that time, even the bees that had left their hives and taken to the woods.

BY September all the vegetation was fast crumbling to a greyish powder, and Nahum feared that the trees would die before the poison was out of the soil. His wife now had spells of terrific screaming, and he and the boys were in a constant state of nervous tension. They shunned people now, and when school opened the boys did not go. But it was Ammi, on one of his rare visits, who first realised that the well water was no longer good. It had an evil taste that was not exactly foetid nor exactly salty, and Ammi advised his friend to dig another well on higher ground to use till the soil was good again. Nahum, however, ignored the warning, for he had by that time become calloused to strange and unpleasant things. He and the boys continued to use the tainted supply, drinking it as listlessly and mechanically as they ate their meagre and ill-cooked meals and did their thankless and monotonous chores through the aimless days. There was something of stolid resignation about them all, as if they walked half in another world between lines of nameless guards to a certain and familiar doom.

(Continued on page 110)

"Extraordinary" is the word best describing the work of **Howard Phillips Lovecraft**. He struggled through his writing career mostly in poverty. While he opened his stories with seemingly ordinary folks, the tales often curved and bent into terror and madness. Like many artists, Lovecraft the pulp-fiction writer became a superstar *after* his death, and his work is the pride and bedrock of horror and fantasy.

H.P. Lovecraft

In a letter to August Derleth (dated Nov. 21, 1930), Lovecraft wrote: "Time, space, and natural law hold for me suggestions of intolerable bondage, and I form no picture of emotional satisfaction which does not involve their defeat — especially the defeat of time, so that one may merge oneself with the whole historic stream and be wholly emancipated from the transient and the ephemeral."

"The Colour Out of Space" fills that description and has been popular among filmmakers. Some adaptations include: *Die, Monster, Die!* (1965), starring Nick Adams; *The Curse* (1987), starring Will Wheaton and Claude Akins, shares the plot of the Lovecraft story; 2008-spawned *Colour from the Dark*, set in Italy, starring Michael Segal; 2010 saw another adaptation called *Die Farbe* (The Color) a black & white Germany film; 2017 came a true name film out of Italy with David Figueiroa and Lucas Ponciano; *Annihilation* (2018) based on Jeff VanderMeer's same-name novel, but coincidentally contained numerous Lovecraft "Colour" similarities; Finally, Rotten Tomatoes bestowed an 86% rating to *Color Out of Space* (2019) starring Nicholas Cage.

— *Audrey Parente*

Thaddeus went mad in September after a visit to the well. He had gone with a pail and had come back empty-handed, shrieking and waving his arms, and sometimes lapsing into an inane titter or a whisper about "the moving colours down there." Two in one family was pretty bad, but Nahum was very brave about it. He let the boy run about for a week until he began stumbling and hurting himself, and then he shut him in an attic room across the hall from his mother's. The way they screamed at each other from behind their locked doors was very terrible, especially to little Merwin, who fancied they talked in some terrible language that was not of earth. Merwin was getting frightfully imaginative, and his restlessness was worse after the shutting away of the brother who had been his greatest playmate.

Almost at the same time the mortality among the livestock commenced. Poultry turned greyish and died very quickly, their meat being found dry and noisome upon cutting. Hogs grew inordinately fat, then suddenly began to undergo loathsome changes which no one could explain. Their meat was of course useless, and Nahum was at his wit's end. No rural veterinary would approach his place, and the city veterinary from Arkham was openly baffled. The swine began growing grey and brittle and falling to pieces before they died, and their eyes and muzzles developed singular alterations. It was very inexplicable, for they had never been fed from the tainted vegetation. Then something struck the cows. Certain areas or sometimes the whole body would be uncannily shrivelled or compressed, and atrocious collapses or disintegrations were common. In the last stages—and death was always the result—there would be a greying and turning brittle like that which beset the hogs. There could be no question of poison, for all the cases occurred in a locked and undisturbed barn. No bites of prowling things could have brought the virus, for what live beast of earth can pass through solid obstacles? It must be only natural disease—yet what disease could wreak such results was beyond any mind's guessing. When the harvest came there was not an animal surviving on the place, for the stock and poultry were dead and the dogs had run away. These dogs, three in number, had all vanished one night and were never heard of again. The five cats had left some time before, but their going was scarcely noticed since there now seemed to be no mice, and only Mrs. Gardner had made pets of the graceful felines.

On the nineteenth of October, Nahum staggered into Ammi's house with hideous news. The death had come to poor Thaddeus in his attic room, and it had come in a way which could not be told. Nahum had dug a grave in the railed family plot behind the farm, and had put therein what he found. There could have been nothing from outside, for the small barred window and locked door were intact; but it was much as it had been in the barn. Ammi and his wife consoled the stricken man as best they could, but shuddered as they did so. Stark terror seemed to cling round the Gardners and all they touched, and the very presence of one in the house was a breath from regions unnamed and unnamable. Ammi accompanied Nahum home with the greatest reluctance, and did what he might to calm the hysterical sobbing of little Merwin. Zenas needed no calming. He had come of late to do nothing but stare into space and obey what his father told him; and Ammi thought that his fate was very merciful. Now and then Merwin's screams were answered faintly from the attic, and in response to an inquiring look Nahum said that his wife was getting very feeble. When night approached, Ammi managed to get away; for not even friendship could make him stay in that spot when the faint glow of the vegetation began and the trees may or may not have swayed without wind. It was really lucky for Ammi that he was not more imaginative. Even as things were, his mind was bent ever so slightly; but had he been able to connect and reflect upon all the portents around him he must inevitably have turned a total maniac. In the twilight he hastened home, the screams of the mad woman and the nervous child ringing horribly in his ears.

THREE days later Nahum lurched into Ammi's kitchen in the early morning, and in the absence of his host stammered out a desperate tale once more, while Mrs. Pierce listened in a clutching fright. It was little Merwin this time. He was gone. He had gone out late at night with a lantern and pail for water, and had never come back. He'd been going to pieces for days, and hardly knew what he was about. Screamed at everything. There had been a frantic shriek from the yard then, but before the father could get to the door, the boy was gone. There was no glow from the lantern he had taken, and of the child himself no trace. At the time Nahum thought the lantern and pail were gone too; but when dawn came, and the man had plodded back from his all-night search of the woods and fields, he had found some very curious things near the well. There was a crushed and apparently somewhat melted mass of iron which had certainly been the lantern; while a bent bail and twisted iron hoops beside it, both half-fused, seemed to hint at the remnants of the pail. That was all. Nahum was past imagining, Mrs. Pierce was blank, and Ammi, when he had reached home and heard the tale, could give no guess. Merwin was gone, and there would be no use in telling the people around, who shunned all Gardners now. No use, either, in telling the city people at Arkham who laughed at everything. Thad was gone, and now Merwin was gone. Something was creeping and creeping and waiting to be seen and felt and heard. Nahum would go soon, and he wanted Ammi to look after his wife and Zenas if they survived him. It must all be a judgment of some sort; though he could not fancy what for, since he had always walked uprightly in the Lord's ways so far as he knew.

For over two weeks Ammi saw nothing of Nahum; and then, worried about what might have happened, he overcame his fears and paid the Gardner place a visit. There was no smoke from the great chimney, and for a moment the visitor was apprehensive of the worst. The aspect of the whole farm was shocking—greyish withered grass and leaves on the ground, vines falling in brittle wreckage from archaic walls and gables, and great bare trees clawing up at the grey November sky with a studied malevolence which Ammi could not but feel had come from some subtle change in the tilt of the branches. But Nahum was alive, after all. He was weak, and lying on a couch in the low-ceiled kitchen, but perfectly conscious and able to give simple orders to Zenas. The room was deadly cold; and as Ammi visibly shivered, the host shouted huskily to Zenas for more wood. Wood, indeed, was sorely needed; since the cavernous fireplace was unlit and empty, with a cloud of soot blowing about in the chill wind that came down the chimney. Presently Nahum asked him if the extra wood had made him any more comfortable, and then Ammi saw what had happened. The stoutest cord had broken at last, and the hapless farmer's mind was proof against more sorrow.

QUESTIONING tactfully, Ammi could get no clear data at all about the missing Zenas. "In the well—he lives in the well—" was all that the clouded father would say. Then there flashed across the visitor's mind a sudden thought of the mad wife, and he changed his line of inquiry. "Nabby? Why, here she is!" was the surprised response of poor Nahum, and Ammi soon saw that he must search for himself. Leaving the harmless babbler on the couch, he took the keys from their nail beside the door and climbed the creaking stairs to the attic. It was very close and noisome up there, and no sound could be heard from any direction. Of the four doors in sight, only one was locked, and on this he tried various keys on the ring he had taken. The third key proved the right one, and after some fumbling Ammi threw open the low white door.

It was quite dark inside, for the window was small and half-obscured by the crude wooden bars; and Ammi could see nothing at all on the wide-planked floor. The stench was beyond enduring, and before proceeding further he had to retreat to another room and return with his lungs filled with breathable air. When he did enter he saw something dark in the corner, and upon seeing it more clearly he screamed outright. While he screamed he thought a momentary cloud eclipsed the window, and a second later he felt himself brushed as if by some hateful current of vapour. Strange colours danced before his eyes; and had not a present horror numbed him he would have thought of the globule in the meteor that the geologist's hammer had shattered, and of the morbid vegetation that had sprouted in the spring. As it was he thought only of the blasphemous monstrosity which confronted him, and which all too clearly had shared the nameless fate of young Thaddeus and the livestock. But the terrible thing about this horror was that it very slowly and perceptibly moved as it continued to crumble.

Ammi would give me no added particulars to this scene, but the shape in the corner does not reappear in his tale as a moving object. There are things which cannot be mentioned, and what is done in common humanity is sometimes cruelly judged by the law. I gathered that no moving thing was left in that attic room, and that to leave anything capable of motion there would have been a deed so monstrous as to damn any accountable being to eternal torment. Anyone but a stolid farmer would have fainted or gone mad, but Ammi walked conscious through that low doorway and locked the accursed secret behind him. There would be Nahum to deal with now; he must be fed and tended, and removed to some place where he could be cared for.

Commencing his descent of the dark stairs, Ammi heard a thud below him. He even thought a scream had been suddenly choked off, and recalled nervously the clammy vapour which had brushed by him in that frightful room above. What presence had his cry and entry started up? Halted by some vague fear, he heard still further sounds below. Indubitably there was a sort of heavy dragging, and a most detestably sticky noise as of some fiendish and unclean species of suction. With an associative sense goaded to feverish heights, he thought unaccountably of what he had seen upstairs. Good God! What eldritch dream-world was this into which he had blundered? He dared move neither backward nor forward, but stood there trembling at the black curve of the boxed-in staircase. Every trifle of the scene burned itself into his brain. The sounds, the sense of dread expectancy, the darkness, the steepness of the narrow steps—and merciful heaven! — the faint but unmistakable luminosity of all the woodwork in sight; steps, sides, exposed laths, and beams alike!

Then there burst forth a frantic whinny from Ammi's horse outside, followed at once by a clatter which told of a frenzied runaway. In another moment horse and buggy had gone beyond earshot, leaving the frightened man on the dark stairs to guess what had sent them. But that was not all. There had been another sound out there. A sort of liquid splash—water—it must have been the well. He had left Hero untied near it, and a buggy-wheel must have brushed the coping and knocked in a stone. And still the pale phosphorescence glowed in that detestably ancient woodwork. God! how old the house was! Most of it built before 1670, and the gambrel roof not later than 1730.

A feeble scratching on the floor downstairs now sounded distinctly, and Ammi's grip tightened on a heavy stick he had picked up in the attic for some purpose. Slowly nerving himself, he finished his descent and walked boldly toward the kitchen. But he did not complete the walk, because what he sought was no longer there. It had come to meet him, and it was still alive after a fashion. Whether it had crawled or whether it had been dragged by any external force, Ammi could not say; but the death had been at it. Everything had happened in the last half-hour, but collapse, greying, and disintegration were already far advanced. There was a horrible brittleness, and dry fragments were scaling off. Ammi could not touch it, but looked horrifiedly into the distorted parody that had been a face. "What was it, Nahum—what was it?" he whispered, and the cleft, bulging lips were just able to crackle out a final answer.

"Nothin' ... nothin' ... the colour ... it burns ... cold an' wet ... but it burns ... it lived in the well ... I seen it ... a kind o' smoke ... jest like the flowers last spring ... the well shone at night ... Thad an' Mernie an' Zenas ... everything alive ... suckin' the life out of everything ... in that stone ... it must a' come in that stone ... pizened the whole place ... dun't know

Commencing his descent of the dark stairs, Ammi heard a thud below him. He even thought a scream had been suddenly choked off ...

what it wants ... that round thing them men from the college dug outen the stone ... they smashed it ... it was that same colour ... jest the same, like the flowers an' plants ... must a' ben more of 'em ... seeds ... seeds ... they growed ... I seen it the fust time this week ... must a' got strong on Zenas ... he was a big boy, full o' life ... it beats down your mind an' then gits ye ... burns ye up ... in the well water ... you was right about that ... evil water ... Zenas never come back from the well ... can't git away ... draws ye ... ye know summ'at's comin', but 'tain't no use ... I seen it time an' agin senct Zenas was took ... whar's Nabby, Ammi? ... my head's no good ... dun't know how long senct I fed her ... it'll git her ef we ain't keerful ... jest a colour ... her face is gettin' to hev that colour sometimes towards night ... an' it burns an' sucks ... it come from some place whar things ain't as they is here ... one o' them professors said so ... he was right ... look out, Ammi, it'll do suthin' more ... sucks the life out. ..."

But that was all. That which spoke could speak no more because it had completely caved in. Ammi laid a red checked tablecloth over what was left and reeled out the back door into the fields. He climbed the slope to the ten-acre pasture and stumbled home by the north road and the woods. He could not pass that well from which his horse had run away. He had looked at it through the window, and had seen that no stone was missing from the rim. Then the lurching buggy had not dislodged anything after all—the splash had been something else—something which went into the well after it had done with poor Nahum....

When Ammi reached his house the horse and buggy had arrived before him and thrown his wife into fits of anxiety. Reassuring her without explanations, he set out at once for Arkham and notified the authorities that the Gardner family was no more. He indulged in no details, but merely told of the deaths of Nahum and Nabby, that of Thaddeus being already known, and mentioned that the cause seemed to be the same strange ailment which had killed the livestock. He also stated that Merwin and Zenas had disappeared. There was considerable questioning at the police station, and in the end Ammi was compelled to take three officers to the Gardner farm, together with the coroner, the medical examiner, and the veterinary who had treated the diseased animals. He went much against his will, for the afternoon was advancing and he feared the fall of night over that accursed place, but it was some comfort to have so many people with him.

The six men drove out in a democrat-wagon, following Ammi's buggy, and arrived at the pest-ridden farmhouse about four o'clock. Used as the officers were to gruesome experiences, not one remained unmoved at what was found in the attic and under the red checked tablecloth on the floor below. The whole aspect of the farm with its grey desolation was terrible enough, but those two crumbling objects were beyond all bounds. No one could look long at them, and even the medical examiner admitted that there was very little to examine. Specimens could be analysed, of course, so he busied himself in obtaining them—and here it develops that a very puzzling aftermath occurred at the college laboratory where the two phials of dust were finally taken. Under the spectroscope both samples gave off an unknown spectrum, in which many of the baffling bands were precisely like those which the strange meteor had yielded in the previous year. The property of emitting this spectrum vanished in a month, the dust thereafter consisting mainly of alkaline phosphates and carbonates.

Ammi would not have told the men about the well if he had thought they meant to do anything then and there. It was getting toward sunset, and he was anxious to be away. But he could not help glancing nervously at the stony curb by the great sweep, and when a detective questioned him he admitted that Nahum had feared something down there—so much so that he had never even thought of searching it for Merwin or Zenas. After that nothing would do but that they empty and explore the well immediately, so Ammi had to wait trembling while pail after pail of rank water was hauled up and splashed on the soaking ground outside. The men sniffed in disgust at the fluid, and toward the last held their noses against the foetor they were uncovering. It was not so long a job as they had feared it would be, since the water was phenomenally low. There is no need to speak too exactly of what they found. Merwin and Zenas were both there, in part, though the vestiges were mainly skeletal. There were also a small deer and a large dog in about the same state, and a number of bones of smaller animals. The ooze and slime at the bottom seemed inexplicably porous and bubbling, and a man who descended on hand-holds with a long pole found that he could sink the wooden shaft to any depth in the mud of the floor without meeting any solid obstruction.

TWILIGHT had now fallen, and lanterns were brought from the house. Then, when it was seen that nothing further could be gained from the well, everyone went indoors and conferred in the ancient sitting-room while the intermittent light of a spectral half-moon played wanly on the grey desolation outside. The men were frankly nonplussed by the entire case, and could find no convincing common element to link the strange vegetable conditions, the unknown disease of livestock and humans, and the unaccountable deaths of Merwin and Zenas in the tainted well. They had heard the common country talk, it is true; but could not believe that anything contrary to natural law had occurred. No doubt the meteor had poisoned the soil, but the illness of persons and animals who had eaten nothing grown in that soil was another matter. Was it the well water? Very possibly. It might be a good idea to analyse it. But what peculiar madness could have made both boys jump into the well? Their deeds were so similar—and the fragments shewed that they had both suffered from the grey brittle death. Why was everything so grey and brittle?

It was the coroner, seated near a window overlooking the yard, who first noticed the glow about the well. Night had fully set in, and all the abhorrent grounds seemed faintly luminous with more than the fitful moonbeams; but this new glow was something definite and distinct, and appeared to shoot up from the black pit like a softened ray from a searchlight, giving dull reflections in the little ground pools where the water had been emptied. It had a very queer colour, and as all the men clustered round the window Ammi gave a violent start. For this strange beam of ghastly miasma was to him of no unfamiliar hue. He had seen that colour before, and feared to think what it might mean. He had seen it in the nasty brittle globule in that aërolite two summers ago, had seen it in the crazy vegetation of the springtime, and had thought he had seen it for an instant that very morning against the small barred window of that terrible attic room where nameless things had happened. It had flashed there a second, and a clammy and hateful current of vapour had brushed past him—and then poor Nahum had been taken by something of that colour. He had said so at the last—said it was the globule and the plants. After that had come the runaway in the yard and the splash in the well—and now that well was belching forth to the night a pale insidious beam of the same daemoniac tint.

It does credit to the alertness of Ammi's mind that he puzzled even at that tense moment over a point which was essentially scientific. He could not but wonder at his gleaning of the same impression from a vapour glimpsed in the daytime, against a window opening on the morning sky, and from a nocturnal exhalation seen as a phosphorescent mist against the black and blasted landscape. It wasn't right—it was against Nature—and he thought of those terrible last words of his stricken friend, "It come from some place whar things ain't as they is here … one o' them professors said so.…"

ALL three horses outside, tied to a pair of shrivelled saplings by the road, were now neighing and pawing frantically. The wagon driver started for the door to do something, but Ammi laid a shaky hand on his shoulder. "Dun't go out thar," he whispered. "They's more to this nor what we know. Nahum said somethin' lived in the well that sucks your life out. He said it must be some'at growed from a round ball like one we all seen in the meteor stone that fell a year ago June. Sucks an' burns, he said, an' is jest a cloud of colour like that light out thar now, that ye can hardly see an' can't tell what it is. Nahum thought it feeds on everything livin' an' gits stronger all the time. He said he seen it this last week. It must be somethin' from away off in the sky like the men from the college last year says the meteor stone was. The way it's made an' the way it works ain't like no way o' God's world. It's some'at from beyond."

SO the men paused indecisively as the light from the well grew stronger and the hitched horses pawed and whinnied in increasing frenzy. It was truly an awful moment; with terror in that ancient and accursed house itself, four monstrous sets of fragments—two from the house and two from the well—in the woodshed behind, and that shaft of unknown and unholy iridescence from the slimy depths in front. Ammi had restrained the driver on impulse, forgetting how uninjured he himself was after the clammy brushing of that coloured vapour in the attic room, but perhaps it is just as well that he acted as he did. No one will ever know what was abroad that night; and though the blasphemy from beyond had not so far hurt any human of unweakened mind, there is no telling what it might not have done at that last moment, and with its seemingly increased strength and the special signs of purpose it was soon to display beneath the half-clouded moonlit sky.

All at once one of the detectives at the window gave a short, sharp gasp. The others looked at him, and then quickly followed his own gaze upward to the point at which its idle straying had been suddenly arrested. There was no need for words. What had been disputed in country gossip was disputable no longer, and it is because of the thing which every man of that party agreed in whispering later on that the strange days are never talked about in Arkham. It is necessary to premise that there was no wind at that hour of the evening. One did arise not long afterward, but there was absolutely none then. Even the dry tips of the lingering hedge-mustard, grey and blighted, and the fringe on the roof of the standing democrat-wagon were unstirred. And yet amid that tense, godless calm the high bare boughs of all the trees in the yard were moving. They were twitching morbidly and spasmodically, clawing in convulsive and epileptic madness at the moonlit clouds; scratching impotently in the noxious air as if jerked by some alien and bodiless line of linkage with subterrene horrors writhing and struggling below the black roots.

NOT a man breathed for several seconds. Then a cloud of darker depth passed over the moon, and the silhouette of clutching branches faded out momentarily. At this there was a general cry; muffled with awe, but husky and almost identical from every throat. For the terror had not faded with the silhouette, and in a fearsome instant of deeper darkness the watchers saw wriggling at that treetop height a thousand tiny points of faint and unhallowed radiance, tipping each bough like the fire of St. Elmo or the flames that came down on the apostles' heads at Pentecost. It was a monstrous constellation of unnatural light, like a glutted swarm of corpse-fed fireflies dancing hellish sarabands over an accursed marsh; and its colour was that same nameless intrusion which Ammi had come to recognise and dread. All the while the shaft of phosphorescence from the well was getting brighter and brighter, bringing to the minds of the huddled men a sense of doom and abnormality which far outraced any image their conscious minds could form. It was no longer shining out, it was pouring out; and as the shapeless stream of unplaceable colour left the well it seemed to flow directly into the sky.

The veterinary shivered, and walked to the front door to drop the heavy extra bar across it. Ammi shook no less, and had to tug and point for lack of a controllable voice when he wished to draw notice to the growing luminosity of the trees. The neighing and stamping of the horses had become utterly frightful, but not a soul of that group in the old house would have ventured forth for any earthly reward. With the moments the shining of the trees increased, while their restless branches seemed to strain more and more toward verticality. The wood of the well-sweep was shining now, and presently a policeman dumbly pointed to some wooden sheds and bee-hives near the stone wall on the west. They were commencing to shine, too, though the tethered vehicles of the visitors seemed so far unaffected. Then there was a wild commotion and clopping in the road, and as Ammi quenched the lamp for better seeing they realised that the span of frantic greys had broke their sapling and run off with the democrat-wagon.

The shock served to loosen several tongues, and embarrassed whispers were exchanged. "It spreads on everything organic that's been around here," muttered the medical examiner. No one replied, but the man who had been in the well gave a hint that his long pole must have stirred up something intangible. "It was awful," he added. "There was no bottom at all. Just ooze and bubbles and the feeling of something lurking under there." Ammi's horse still pawed and screamed deafeningly in the road outside, and nearly drowned its owner's faint quaver as he mumbled his formless reflections. "It come from that stone ... it growed down thar ... it got everything livin' ... it fed itself on 'em, mind and body ... Thad an' Mernie, Zenas an' Nabby ... Nahum was the last ... they all drunk the water ... it got strong on 'em ... it come from beyond, whar things ain't like they be here ... now it's goin' home ..."

At this point, as the column of unknown colour flared suddenly stronger and began to weave itself into fantastic suggestions of shape which each spectator later described differently, there came from poor tethered Hero such a sound as no man before or since ever heard from a horse. Every person in that low-pitched sitting room stopped his ears, and Ammi turned away from the window in horror and nausea. Words could not convey it—when Ammi looked out again the hapless beast lay huddled inert on the moonlit ground between the splintered shafts of the buggy. That was the last of Hero till they buried him next day. But the present was no time to mourn, for almost at this instant a detective silently called attention to something terrible in the very room with them. In the absence of the lamplight it was clear that a faint phosphorescence had begun to pervade the entire apartment. It glowed on the broad-planked floor and the fragment of rag carpet, and shimmered over the sashes of the small-paned windows. It ran up and down the exposed corner-posts, coruscated about the shelf and mantel, and infected the very doors and furniture. Each minute saw it strengthen, and at last it was very plain that healthy living things must leave that house.

Ammi shewed them the back door and the path up through the fields to the ten-acre pasture. They walked and stumbled as in a dream, and did not dare look back till they were far away on the high ground. They were glad of the path, for they could not have gone the front way, by that well. It was bad enough passing the glowing barn and sheds, and those shining orchard trees with their gnarled, fiendish contours; but thank heaven the branches did their worst twisting high up. The moon went under some very black clouds as they crossed the rustic bridge over Chapman's Brook, and it was blind groping from there to the open meadows.

WHEN they looked back toward the valley and the distant Gardner place at the bottom they saw a fearsome sight. All the farm was shining with the hideous unknown blend of colour; trees, buildings, and even such grass and herbage as had not been wholly changed to lethal grey brittleness. The boughs were all straining skyward, tipped with tongues of foul flame, and lambent tricklings of the same monstrous fire were creeping about the ridgepoles of the house, barn, and sheds. It was a scene from a vision of Fuseli, and over all the rest reigned that riot of luminous amorphousness, that alien and undimensioned rainbow of cryptic poison from the well—seething, feeling, lapping, reaching, scintillating, straining, and malignly bubbling in its cosmic and unrecognisable chromaticism.

Then without warning the hideous thing shot vertically up toward the sky like a rocket or meteor, leaving behind no trail and disappearing through a round and curiously regular hole in the clouds before any man could gasp or cry out. No watcher can ever forget that sight, and Ammi stared blankly at the stars of Cygnus, Deneb twinkling above the others, where the unknown colour had melted into the Milky Way. But his gaze was the next moment called swiftly to earth by the crackling in the valley. It was just that. Only a wooden ripping and crackling, and not an explosion, as so many others of the party vowed. Yet the outcome was the same, for in one feverish, kaleidoscopic instant there burst up from that doomed and accursed farm a gleamingly eruptive cataclysm of unnatural sparks and substance; blurring the glance of the few who saw it, and sending forth to the zenith a bombarding cloudburst of such coloured and fantastic fragments as our universe must needs disown. Through quickly reclosing vapours they followed the great morbidity that had vanished, and in another second they had vanished too. Behind and below was only a darkness to which the men dared not return, and all about was a mounting wind which seemed to sweep down in black, frore gusts from interstellar space. It shrieked and howled, and lashed the fields and distorted woods in a mad cosmic frenzy, till soon the trembling party realised it would be no use waiting for the moon to shew what was left down there at Nahum's.

Too awed even to hint theories, the seven shaking men trudged back toward Arkham by the north road. Ammi was worse than his fellows, and begged them to see him inside his own kitchen, instead of keeping straight on to town. He did not wish to cross the nighted, wind-whipped woods alone to his home on the main road. For he had had an added shock that the others were spared, and was crushed forever with a brooding fear he dared not even mention for many years to come. As the rest of the watchers on that tempestuous hill had stolidly set their faces toward the road, Ammi had looked back an instant at the shadowed valley of desolation so lately sheltering his ill-starred friend. And from that stricken, far-away spot he had seen something feebly rise, only to sink down again upon the place from which the great shapeless horror had shot into the sky. It was just a colour—but not any colour of our earth or heavens. And because Ammi recognised that colour, and knew that this last faint remnant must still lurk down there in the well, he has never been quite right since.

Ammi would never go near the place again. It is over half a century now since the horror happened, but he has never been there, and will be glad when the new reservoir blots it out. I shall be glad, too, for I do not like the way the sunlight changed colour around the mouth of that abandoned well I passed. I hope the water will always be very deep—but even so, I shall never drink it. I do not think I shall visit the Arkham country hereafter. Three of the men who had been with Ammi returned the next morning to see the ruins by daylight, but there were not any real ruins. Only the bricks of the chimney, the stones of the cellar, some mineral and metallic litter here and there, and the rim of that nefandous well. Save for Ammi's dead horse, which they towed away and buried, and the buggy which they shortly returned to him, everything that had ever been living had gone. Five eldritch acres of dusty grey desert remained, nor has anything ever grown there since. To this day it sprawls open to the sky like a great spot eaten by acid in the woods and fields, and the few who have ever dared glimpse it in spite of the rural tales have named it "the blasted heath".

The rural tales are queer. They might be even queerer if city men and college chemists could be interested enough to analyse the water from that disused well, or the grey dust that no wind seems ever to disperse. Botanists, too, ought to study the stunted flora on the borders of that spot, for they might shed light on the country notion that the blight is spreading—little by little, perhaps an inch a year. People say the colour of the neighbouring herbage is not quite right in the spring, and that wild things leave queer prints in the light winter snow. Snow never seems quite so heavy on the blasted heath as it is elsewhere. Horses—the few that are left in this motor age—grow skittish in the silent valley; and hunters cannot depend on their dogs too near the splotch of greyish dust.

They say the mental influences are very bad, too. Numbers went queer in the years after Nahum's taking, and always they lacked the power to get away. Then the stronger-minded folk all left the region, and only the foreigners tried to live in the crumbling old homesteads. They could not stay, though; and one sometimes wonders

(Continued on page 135)

Theft of the Crown Jewels

A Shep Malloy Story
By JOHN CLEMONS

*Before the Very Eyes
of a Lawman, a Dastardly Swindle
in Stones Takes Shape!*

IN the ballroom everyone was merry; it was noisy, crowded, alive with lights and life and laughter. All were eager to hear the playing of the great Sigourney.

As the hunchbacked figure at the piano sat chafing his wrists and dry-washing his hands, a slender woman detached herself from the circle of the transported faces and wended her way toward him. The man at the piano recognized her at once as a princess of old Czarist Russia who, at the time of her country's great upheaval, had managed to escape with innumerable, priceless jewels of the royal family. A tall, monocled gentleman edged close to the princess. The pianist recognized the monocled gentleman also; knew him for an impostor, a fraud who called himself Count Debussy; a sinister character who had tested the mettle of the police of many countries but had thus far emerged victorious. And this shady character was paying court to the lady who wore the crown jewels!

The musician lent his genius to an interpretation of the romantic "Intermezzi," by Brahms. He brought out the sonorous qualities of the keyboard with perhaps a little more fervor and slightly more drama than the composer intended, handling the massed tones with a vast fullness, making a rippling cascade of the gracious runs.

Intent upon the intricate score, he failed to heed the ominous rumbling of his audience, until presently he was aware of a pair of weird eyes that peered at him over the piano's low rim; of a twisted form, of a forbidding, distorted countenance.

HIS efforts suddenly lost all purpose; ceased abruptly in a harsh medley of broken chords! The great room was all at once a hive of excitement; for, confronting the pianist, was a living breathing, hostile image of himself.

The newcomer leveled a shaking forefinger at the man seated at the piano.

"Impostor!" he denounced in a throaty bass that carried to the farthermost corners. "You dare take my place! *My* place — *me — the great Sigourney!*"

The man who had been playing with the skill of a master indulged in a fleeting, one-sided smile.

"I didn't do so badly," he remarked coolly. "Quite well, in fact, don't you think? At least I did better at the piano than the ropes I bound you with!"

The startled audience seemed averse to quick action. The newcomer stormed hoarsely, "This man is Shep Malloy!"

And as if mere mention of Malloy, the master crook, were a signal for shadowy legerdemain — the lights went out!

At once Malloy realized that someone — likely Debussy — was taking advantage of the disturbance created by the genuine Sigourney's dramatic accusation, to further illicit ends. For the known presence of Malloy would be made to account for whatever deviltry the ingenious Debussy had planned.

Malloy heard labored breathing close to him and knew instinctively it was the fake count. He strained his eyes toward where he knew the princess stood, saw the quick glint of fiery jewels. Then — the false noble *was* robbing the princess!

Any moment the lights might go on, and without further reflection, the master crook pounced upon the fake nobleman. A well-directed blow to the base of the skull dropped Debussy. Malloy heaved him on one shoulder, dropped through the half-open French doors behind the piano, a few inches to the soft lawn below.

It was several precious minutes before the lighting trouble was located and a new fuse inserted. When at length the lights went on, the princess was standing there, her round eyes reflecting a great fear. She was stripped bare of her precious jewels!

At once two other things were apparent. Debussy was gone, and so was Shep Malloy!

Malloy smiled as he reached his parked Rolls in the shadow of a spreading elm. The guise of Sigourney had been his passport to the fabulous estate. But now the disguise had outlived its usefulness. Hastily, Malloy changed his clothes from an ample store in his car.

The master crook sported a monocle and assumed an attitude of great aloofness as he solemnly joined in the search for the criminal!

They found Debussy at last; he was stretched full length under a hedge, bound and gagged with his own clothing. But

Malloy — and the jewels — were definitely gone.

It was naturally assumed that Debussy, because of his proximity, had witnessed the robbery and rashly attempted to capture the notorious Malloy singlehanded. Thus, automatically, Debussy, the bogus nobleman, crook, actually became a hero!

But only one man in the country would know this, that Shep Malloy was the hero; only one man accorded Malloy the respect due him. This was the chief of Department of Justice agents at Washington; the man who had sent him this night on the trail of Debussy, a notorious swindler, and blackguard of international repute. For Shep Malloy was a Secret Service agent, a daredevil who had voluntarily branded himself an underworld character to further the ends of justice. To reveal his secret would spell *finis* to the marked usefulness of the carefully built-up desperado known as the formidable Shep Malloy.

Now, although in possession of the stolen jewels, a serious problem faced the Government man. He must somehow manage not only to return the jewels to their rightful owner, but also to unmask the fake count and place him in the toils of the law.

Then, too, he was confronted with the business of guarding against further depredations. Undoubtedly the count had accomplices, else how account for the lights going out at the crucial moment?

Malloy's first concern on returning to the ball, was not so much the rounding up of Count Debussy and his gang as the gathering of evidence to convict them — a feat that had baffled the police of two continents. He proceeded at once to seek out Debussy and insinuate himself into the fake noble's good graces.

Malloy found Debussy glum and taciturn, unresponsive to his friendly overtures. Fearful of arousing the other's suspicion, Malloy was forced to desist from that line of action. Not, however, before he had made one momentous discovery; the count was to be an overnight guest at the estate.

Posing as Debussy, Malloy ascertained the count's room by a telephoned query to the housekeeper. What safer hiding place for the crown jewels, he reasoned, than in the crook's own room? The Government man hastened to avail himself of the opportunity to secrete the jewels, and returned at once to the ballroom.

At length the guests began to leave. When finally the count was ready to retire — not to sleep, but to plan and plunder — Malloy preceded him to his room by a scant few moments. He hid himself behind a screen and calmly awaited the bogus nobleman's arrival.

Count Debussy opened the door and closed it softly. He lit a small night lamp, and by its feeble rays Malloy watched him remove his long-tailed coat and put on a silk robe. Then the count lit a cigarette and commenced to pace the floor restlessly.

Suddenly there was a soft knock at the door. Instantly the count glided forward, one hand held suggestively in the pocket of his silk gown. He opened the door warily, then threw it wide. A woman entered. And Malloy's amazed eyes told him—it was the princess!

She held the count firmly in an agitated grasp and searched his eyes earnestly.

Originally Published In
Thrilling Detective, Oct. 1935.
Standard Magazines.

"What happened?" she gasped excitedly. "Oh, what have you done?"

The count shook her off savagely.

"What have *I* done, little fool? How was I to know that the pianist was a thief of the first water! We shall have to be contented with the insurance money alone." The count's low chuckle contained no quality of mirth. "We shall at least have earned it—honestly!"

THE truth dawned on Malloy. The secret agent had chanced upon an international ring of crime specialists engaged in the remunerativeart of defrauding prosperous insurance companies. The princess was genuine enough and accounted for Debussy's *entre* into the cream of society. The suave count, working in concert with seemingly burglarized persons, was himself safe as a church — a fact which many puzzled police had reluctantly admitted.

"Come, my dear," whispered Debussy, his voice suddenly soft, persuasive. "There's much to be done. Tonight, this dark old house holds riches beyond the dreams of avarice." He tensed all at once; his brows lifted slowly so that the monocle fell away and dangled unheeded. "You don't — suspect *me* — surely!"

The princess' pained eyes roved restlessly, a great uncertainty plainly visible in them.

Without warning the door was flung violently open. A huge, bearded man strode across the room, angrily wrenching the girl away before he turned to close the door.

"Tanya," he whispered in a subdued rumble, "Debussy has tricked us. What have I told you all along — the man is a common thief and not to be trusted!"

"I beg your pardon!" Debussy blazed.

"Alexis — please!" begged the princess.

But Alexis was harsh. "Quick! What have you done with the crown jewels!" he demanded of the count.

"I tell you Shep Malloy stole them—"

"What fantastic lie have you concocted?" the newcomer snarled. "Who is this accomplice of yours?"

And in his hiding place Malloy found cause to worry. He had not counted on a falling out among the thieves. The Government man prayed the quarrel would not lead to a thorough search of the count's room.

He watched Debussy's face grow stony, saw his eyes narrow. The count lit a cigarette with fine disdain, blew a cloud of smoke and eyed his tormentor coldly.

"You shall have to be satisfied with the insurance money alone," he said in measured tones. "The jewels are definitely stolen."

"Insurance money!" choked the other through his short beard. "Did you hear that, my sister? Insurance money! — Why, those jewels were my family heirlooms! Do you think any amount of money shall ever compensate for their loss!"

He took a threatening step forward. His eyes glowered; his bull neck tensed. And then Debussy whipped out a pistol.

The new turn of events alarmed Malloy afresh. Save for the snub-nosed pocket pistol which he carried — unloaded — the secret agent was unarmed. And the State could demand no satisfaction from a dead criminal!

"You see, my sister," said the big man thickly, "he was expecting trouble with me. It is the same as admitting his guilt!"

The count nodded slowly. "I was expecting trouble with you," he admitted.

"Because you're guilty of cheating us," persisted Alexis. "Because you are a jackal — a common thief!"

"You are as deeply involved as I," Debussy reminded him coolly.

"I do not have a pistol," confessed the big man, "but — Bah!" With a sudden movement amazingly quick for a man of his bulk, the princess' brother knocked the gun from Debussy's grasp and caught the hapless pseudo noble by the throat with one great paw. The gun landed so close to Malloy that he could reach out and grab it.

Malloy would serve his ends better by remaining in hiding, yet he could not stand by and watch a man — even a criminal — murdered. But before he could make a definite move the princess leaped between the two men. At once Malloy stooped, hurriedly secured the count's pistol. A half minute later he quietly slipped it back where it had fallen.

The antagonists stood crouched, panting, wiping the sweat from their red faces. The ghostly rays from the little night light reflected murder in their wild eyes.

"Fools!" hissed the princess. "Do you wish to awaken the entire household?"

The two men straightened at the warning. The count stuck the monocle in his eye and fixed his tie.

"There is work to be done," he said, addressing his late adversary. "We shall adjust our differences later," he added significantly.

The big man nodded his leonine head slowly.

"We shall," he promised grimly.

The count searched for his pistol, found it in a dark corner. Then he removed his silk gown and slipped into his long-tailed coat. The men adjusted their monocles, squared their shoulders. The handsome trio stood ready to embark on their pilgrimage of plunder.

"I don't like this," protested the big man suddenly. "This was not in the bargain."

"Neither do I," admitted the princess frowning. "It's common thievery."

"So is the insurance game," the count reminded her.

"But that was merely a—a swindle," Alexis argued.

"And — and different," his sister added a little desperately.

"Just the same, my princess, the law frowns upon it," retorted the count with fine sarcasm. "What you really mean," he continued, leering from one to the other of the tense faces, "is that you took few chances. Now, with an opportunity to recoup our loss of the crown jewels, you're afraid!"

The count's thrust went home. The latent fire in the woman's eyes burst into flame. Her brother shook with a fierce hurt pride.

"Come along," he choked. "We'll go with you, Debussy." He took his sister's arm. The three made for the door. Then—

A discreet cough from somewhere in the room froze them in mid-stride. Slowly the trio turned — to confront a tall man in evening clothes, nonchalantly lighting a cigarette. In a flash the count had the intruder covered with his pistol. He recognized him at once as the distinguished gentleman whose friendly advances, he had earlier repulsed.

"Who are you?" Debussy demanded fiercely. "What are you doing here!"

The intruder arched fine brows. If Alexis continued to believe that the count was in league with Malloy, it would help the police in breaking down the trio in the event that they were captured. The stranger said in well feigned surprise:

"Surely, my dear count, you do not repudiate your partner in crime — Shep Malloy!"

The princess' hand flew to her trembling mouth. Her brother blinked stupidly. But not so the count. He took deliberate aim and fired.

Only a metallic click answered him. Again and again he pulled the trigger, frantically, desperately.

"I took the precaution to empty your pistol," Malloy smiled easily. "While you three were preoccupied —"

"You mean you heard — you saw — everything?" breathed the princess.

Malloy exhaled luxuriously; his shrug was more eloquent than words.

Alexis turned on the count in frigid wrath.

"You swine," he spat, "you've destroyed us utterly!" He faced Malloy. "You have the jewels?" he asked anxiously.

"I have the jewels," Malloy replied, "and a revolver. I have hidden the jewels," he continued, "but the reVolver — " It gleamed in his hand very suddenly.

"If you have hidden the jewels," Alexis whispered hoarsely, "you don't need a revolver. We are completely in your power."

Malloy nodded toward the white-faced, outraged count. Alexis interpreted the nod correctly.

"Don't worry," the big man growled. "I'll take care of him."

This was better than Malloy had dared hope for; the Princess Tanya and her brother Alexis would submit peacefully because Malloy had their precious family jewels, and big Alexis would keep Count Debussy subdued because he thought him a traitor.

"Now," Alexis asked tensely, "what is

your price — how much for the crown jewels?"

"First," said the secret agent, his voice rising, "let me ask you what chance I have to collect."

The Government man was sparring for time. He wanted an opportunity to stage a denouement of the trio before witnesses.

"You're talking too loudly," cautioned the princess. "You'll bring the police! There must be a score about!"

Which was, of course, Malloy's sole intention. He knew that before breaking in, the police would doubtless listen at the door to determine the cause of the disturbance. He intended to let them hear enough to convict the conspirators.

The secret agent heard a soft footstep at the door. Perhaps the police had arrived attracted by the unseemly commotion; the grounds were swarming with detectives since the theft of the crown jewels.

"How do I know you have enough money to buy back the jewels?" he fairly shouted.

"Please! Please, be quiet!" the princess entreated,

"If you are not penniless," Malloy shouted relentlessly, "why should you enter into an alliance with this fake count, Debussy, to swindle the insurance people by allowing him to steal the jewels — later collecting both the insurance money and the jewels!"

Debussy glowered, his face was contorted with rage.

"Quiet," he gritted.

"Quiet? Why should I be quiet," Malloy retorted. "I am an honorable crook and admit it. You go about — a poseur, a fake, insinuating yourself in honest people's good graces and then double crossing them.

"You have never been convinced because always the people whose jewels were stolen have been a party to the crime. You split the insurance money but inevitably you made off with the jewels in the end. The actual owners were gagged by the fear of exposure if they should attempt reprisal!"

"Quiet!" roared Debussy in a rage beyond control. The princess sobbed quietly, her head in her hands. Big Alexis grimaced with remorse and self-accusation. His big fists clenched and unclenched in white-hot anger.

A sudden frenzy seized Debussy, broke all outward signs of gentility. He took a tentative step toward his tormentor. Malloy had only his impotent pistol, yet he attempted to bluff it out. But the leveled weapon failed to stop the charging desperate crook. Alexis made ready to join the affray.

Just as Malloy came to grips with Debussy, a shout was heard. Instantly the door crashed open, the windows spilled men. Another moment and the lights flashed on. Half a dozen stalwart minions of the law had the little group covered!

The count was dragged off Malloy. Smiling, the Government agent dropped his pistol. He had accomplished his purpose.

The detectives manacled their prisoners' hands. And now a new terror beset the Government operative. He faced, not so much the dread thought of being jailed, but the prospect of being unmasked, of being exposed as on the side of the law, ending forever his usefulness in the underworld as star undercover man.

The detective sergeant who had engineered the coup, addressed Malloy.

"What I want to know," he said, "is where you've hidden the crown jewels."

Now that he had captured the quartet, the detective-sergeant had decided it would not look bad for the record books if he succeeded in retrieving the loot as well. Then too, it would be gratifying if the insurance company included him in the roster of those who deserved liberal reward.

Malloy's only answer was a faintly derisive smile. The jewels were the ace in the Government man's sleeve. He resolved to play accordingly.

The detective wheedled softly: "Come on, Malloy, the jig is up. I was behind the door with my men. We heard everything. Got enough to convict the lot of you."

Still Mallory smiled.

"Tell you what," the detective persisted. "Tell me where you hid the jewels and I'll pull some strings for you."

Malloy looked interested and the detective pressed his advantage. "I'll get you better than an even break," he coaxed smoothly.

Malloy frowned: he seemed on the verge of capitulation. "If it's all the same to you, sergeant," he suggested, "I'd like to talk to you alone."

The detective heave a deep satisfied sigh. At a signal from him, his men marched their prisoners out, closed the door and waited.

Malloy and the detective-sergeant faced each other, the former manacled, helpless; his captor alert, armed, expectant — and a force of armed men on the other side of the door.

Malloy said suavely, smiling, "May I trouble you for a cigarette, my dear fellow?"

The detective recognized, in the apparently prosaic request, a challenge which he readily accepted. The officer's eyes narrowed with caution as he produced his cigarette case. He took a step forward, then stopped suddenly. Malloy was handcuffed, true, but many were the stories bruited about concerning the master crook's uncanny escape tricks. With a decisive shake of the head the detective pocketed his cigarettes.

Malloy's smile broadened, for the officer had taken a forward step before he withdrew the proffered cigarettes, and that was part of Malloy's plan. Now the government man took a backward step and instinctively the detective came forward again.

Inwardly Malloy cheered. For the Government man had maneuvered the detective so that the latter now stood on the tail end of a huge polar bear rug.

The detective said softly, "Come on, Malloy. Tell me where you hid the jewels and I'll make it all right with you. Give you a chance to turn State's evidence, if you want to."

"All right," Malloy said nodding. "It's a go!" he stooped suddenly. The officer's finger tensed on the trigger of his gun. If this was a trick Malloy would never live through it, the detective resolved.

But Malloy's manacled hands went into the gaping mouth of the polar bear's head and came out with a diamond tiara!

In the half-light the thing sparkled like a million frantic and imprisoned sunbeams. The detective gaped, wide-eyed and breathless.

Malloy's hand shot forward again without pause. But this time he grabbed the bear's heavy snout, gave a swift jerk with his two strong hands. The bear rug shot forward on the polished floor, threw the unprepared and unsuspecting detective off his feet!

The officer released his weapon automatically as he fell. At once Malloy smothered the fallen man with his own body, and secured the detective's gun. The two gained their feet, the gun buried in the detective's ample stomach.

There was a loud knocking as vague sounds of the scuffle reached the ears of the listeners at the door. Malloy's weapon dug into the other's midriff. In the face of the deadly pistol the detective had no choice.

"It's all right," shouted the officer. "Just giving him a little third degree," he added at Malloy's whispered suggestion,

Malloy frisked the detective hurriedly; found the detective's keys.

"Quick!" snapped the Government operative. "I'm a desperate man! Fit the key into these handcuffs! And if you fumble, or call those others — "

But the detective was not foolhardy; a desperate man with a weapon is not to be trifled with. With a deft twist he unlocked the manacles. With the handcuffs the Government man locked the detective to a radiator pipe. He gagged the man with the detective's handkerchief. He switched off the lights and vanished through an open window.

Malloy knew he was not yet safe, for the gates would this time be well guarded. True, he could scale a retaining wall and be off, but without a car he would be easy prey for a posse. He sped to his fast Rolls underneath the elm tree. He slid behind the wheel, stepped on the starter, and under his careful guidance the delicately adjusted Rolls glided noiselessly away.

At the gate it was as he had feared; a stout chain barred the path. A uniformed estate guard came on the run from the little gate-house, a business-like gun at the ready.

Malloy stuck out his hand hastily, and in the soft moonglow the guard caught the glint of something metallic, in the out-stretched palm; something gleaming, like the flash of a detective's badge.

"I'm Kennedy, from Headquarters," the Government man rasped. "Quick! Let down the chain! We've just got Shep Malloy!"

With a quick "Yes, sir!" the guard sprang to obey. The heavy chain clanked down.

As Malloy's big car smashed through the breach and gained the freedom of the main highway, he glanced at the shining wafer in his hand and laughed softly.

It was the detective-sergeant's own police shield. ∎

PULPS! COMICS! PAPERBACKS! MORE!
Visit the Vintage Vault section! www.boldventurepress.com

Kali Curse
(Continued from page 90)

carnage all around me with the moans of the wounded Indians and the dead dancer at my feet.

"Sahib Captain," a voice came to me from the darkness.

I spun to see the wizened beggar from outside the Blue Mongoose step from the shadows by one of the deity statues. He was different, however, more upright and his steps were almost regal in his progression.

"You," I said, "how — ?"

"You were the one who could be taught," the old man said. "You were the one who stayed your hand to violence in the Blue Mongoose and even here until it was forced on you."

"I don't understand."

The old man began to waver before my eyes like a column of smoke and his skin tinged blue. "Compassion and love are the utmost powers in the universe," the old man said in a now booming voice that seemed to come from everywhere. "You have resisted the bestial urges of your fellows and so you are the hope for understanding between worlds."

He began to grow taller and wider till he assumed a size that almost touched the ceiling. His rags were gone and he was no longer old, but a perfectly formed, blue skinned figure of classically beautiful form.

"Krishna!" I murmured, stepping back from the Hindu God who stood before me.

He smiled benevolently and waved a hand at my unconscious comrades.

"Teach the others, be a light in the darkness."

"I will," I whispered.

The giant wavered and began to dissolve truly like smoke and blow away, his voice faded even as he did. Then the awesome figure was gone and I was alone with my mates wondering how I was going to do as I promised and help them be better men and to explain to them what I had seen. I was not really sure I had even seen it, but then, that, in a nutshell, describes the very real mystery that was India. ∎

FROM TEEL JAMES GLENN, THE SCI-MAGICKAL WORD OF 1920 EUROPE

The Great War ends in record time through Doktor Mabon's mix of ancient and modern knowledge — steambot servants, great floating dirigibles — and bizarre animal-human hybrids from a secret island. Dark forces conspire to claim these discoveries for their ends, and The Clockwork Nutcracker must halt The Baron's deadly plans to prevent the *next* Great War!

CLOCKWORK NUTCRACKER / from Pro Se Productions

Thubway Tham's

(Continued from page 21)

get my old room if I can, and then—"

"And then you'll be up to your old tricks, eh?"

"Maybe you had better wait," Tham said angrily. "Maybe you had better wait until I do thomething to give you cauthe to talk that way to me. You make me thick, Craddock! Give me that bag!"

Tham took it from him and led the way down the street.

"Why not take the subway from Grand Central?" Craddock asked.

"Well, by heaventh! I have been away for more than a year, and I want to thee the old town!" Tham replied. "I am going to walk to Timeth Thquare and take a train there."

"Well, I'll not pester you just now, Tham," Craddock said. "But I'll be watching you, old boy. And one of these days I'll nab you, and get you right. Then it will be up the river for you."

"Tho? When that day cometh, it will mean that I am thlowin' up," Tham said. "You couldn't catch a cold, Craddock. Thankth, however, for not pethterin' me to-day."

"Don't mention it, Tham."

"And thankth, altho, for carryin' my bag," Thubway Tham added. "You are very kind. Thith ith a good bag."

"And you've probably got one shirt, a couple of collars and a pair of socks in it, even if you do happen to have a good front," Craddock said, laughing.

"Perhapth," said Tham. "A man muth run a bluff onthe in a while, muthn't he? He muth!"

And Thubway Tham, now in the city officially, and safe for the present, hurried on up the street.

When he had gone half a block and was sure that Craddock was not following, he began, to chuckle.

"The thilly ath!" he said. "Right under hith nothe!" ∎

"I HATE CRIME!"

A two-fisted private investigator makes himself a moving target in the concrete and steel jungle of Manhattan. Two-fisted action by DON HARING, in the tradition of Mike Hammer and Shell Scott!

LARRY KENT, P.I.™

LARRY KENT & "I HATE CRIME!" TM Cleveland Publishing, Inc. All Rights reserved.

Wayne Morgan ...

An honest cowpoke searched for his rightful place in the American west ... before he learned abiding by the law doesn't always work for the law-abiding people.

The Masked Rider ...

The mysterious rider who, aided by his friend Blue Hawk, opposes rustlers, land barons, bandits, claim-jumpers, and other assorted lawless men ... *when hangin's too good for them ...*

Western action quarterly

WWW.BOLDVENTUREPRESS.COM

MASKED RIDER WESTERN TM Bold Venture Press. All Rights reserved.

Space Burial

(Continued from page 37)

her arms about his neck, her bosom crushed against him. Faster and faster, till Bill was compelled to move the indicator back and check the speed. Now he and Ursula were floating beside their ship. Bill reached up and grasped the fin, hooked one arm about it, and, with an immense effort, hauled Ursula after him.

They plunged through the lock and stumbled into the empty interior. They dropped, exhausted.

Leaving Ursula there, Bill tottered to the optoscope. Turning it, he saw the phantom trail of Jeribald's ship, thousands of miles away.

A trail of light, cut off at the extremity of the atmosphere of Nestor. Jeribald was heading straight for Jupiter.

And suddenly Bill understood. Vulcan had overheard, with the supreme auditory faculty of his race. Or, if he hadn't overheard, he had determined that they should all share a common fate. The faithful black man had jammed the g. e. control, rendering the ship unmanageable. The pull of Jupiter had had no counterpoise of Jonesite gas. It was the same as if he had shut off the flow in his own little gas gauge.

Space-burial for Jeribald and Astra and Garrou!

But Bill didn't like to think about the nectarines aboard.

He started his engine, turned about, set a course for Earth, and lashed the wheel.

Then he went back to Ursula. And, in the tightening grip of her white arms, he managed to forget all else. ∎

The Robbers
(Continued from page 52)

the long climb up from savagery. How to live on the land, to make do with what they have, to kill in order to survive."

He smiled at the young man's instinctive recoil. "That was perhaps the hardest lesson of all. Civilisation now does not admit of the concept of killing. Earth has been too-well tamed and men have made a fetish of peace. But colonists can't afford to be squeamish. Their lives and those of their children may depend on killing the local fauna — and there is another reason."

"Yes?"

"Survival is struggle. Continual struggle against the entire universe, and, in order to survive, men must be prepared to kill. So that is the plan. There are women, of course. They are being trained how to weave cloth from fur and vegetable fibres, to nurse and to look after their young. We aren't sending you out helpless against a new environment — you have been taught hypnotically and your body has been trained to the ultimate. Hypnotism will enable you to kill each other's pain so that operations and childbirth will be painless. You will have tools, saws, axes, knives, and you will have books and other essentials. But you will have nothing on which you are totally dependent. You will strike roots into the ground and master your environment — or it will master you."

Tony nodded, his mind full of the bright adventure ahead and, as he left the office, his steps were light and his worries a thing of the past. Gerard sighed as he turned towards the psychologist.

"Are we being fair to them, French? Are we being fair to Earth?"

"I know what you mean," said the psychologist quietly. "But to me it isn't a question of fairness. I know that we are draining Earth of all its best and youngest, sapping its vitality by stealing away the very blood and attributes which could save her from senile decay. I know too that we are dumping small groups on a hundred worlds and leaving them there to survive or perish, to live or die, according to whether the planet proves too hostile for them to adapt. But what can we do? Even with the ultra-drive it takes too long to reach the stars and space is so big. A ship can call perhaps once every ten years, and will so call, but more than that is impossible. We must use these young people as our test guides. If they live they have gained a world and so has the race. If they die then they are lost and we try elsewhere. But one thing is certain. While we seed the race among the stars it will never die. Even though they forget all they know and revert back a hundred thousand years until they shiver in their fireless caves and grovel in the dirt for food, yet will the race survive. Nothing matters once we have seeded the stars, nothing can touch the race of man, and that proud monkey will be safe until the end of time. The galaxy is ours, Gerard, all ours, and if we have to rob Earth of all that is best — isn't it worth it?"

The commander nodded, thinking of the boy who had so shortly left them, of his life and what it would be, and of the brave destiny which, all unknowing, he carried with him.

A destiny which was worth any man living a lie. ■

Great Caesar's Ghost

(Continued from page 97)

coins. Among other items, I found a story about a first century coin that had recently netted over three quarters of a million dollars at auction. The image of Caesar Augustus was visible on one side and a large bull on the other.

The hairs on my neck stood and saluted.

***

I don't remember too many of the particulars regarding the next several hours. I do know that I went back downstairs and coaxed a shovel and spade on one of the shelves out of retirement, and found them invaluable assets in my quest for what I hoped might be at least a runner up for the Holy Grail.

Several feet below ground level, beneath the pile of olive leaves in the corner, I found a small, rusted case which I can only guess either my uncle or the previous owner had hidden for safekeeping.

My fingers trembled and I broke a fingernail by the time I finally got that little metal box opened. Inside was a small coin, heavily dust-laden, a monetary orphan lost and lonely for hundreds of centuries. I blew away the dust, rubbed the coin's face with a dirty thumb, blinked and then gasped in awe as I saw on the face of the coin in my hand, the silhouette of Caesar Augustus. On the other side of the coin, the image of a large bull stood out in bold relief.

My mouth outpaced my mind as I involuntarily exclaimed:

"Great Caesar's Ghost!" ∎

Color Out of Space

(Continued from page 120)

what insight beyond ours their wild, weird stores of whispered magic have given them. Their dreams at night, they protest, are very horrible in that grotesque country; and surely the very look of the dark realm is enough to stir a morbid fancy. No traveller has ever escaped a sense of strangeness in those deep ravines, and artists shiver as they paint thick woods whose mystery is as much of the spirit as of the eye. I myself am curious about the sensation I derived from my one lone walk before Ammi told me his tale. When twilight came I had vaguely wished some clouds would gather, for an odd timidity about the deep skyey voids above had crept into my soul.

Do not ask me for my opinion. I do not know—that is all. There was no one but Ammi to question; for Arkham people will not talk about the strange days, and all three professors who saw the aërolite and its coloured globule are dead. There were other globules—depend upon that. One must have fed itself and escaped, and probably there was another which was too late. No doubt it is still down the well—I know there was something wrong with the sunlight I saw above that miasmal brink. The rustics say the blight creeps an inch a year, so perhaps there is a kind of growth or nourishment even now. But whatever daemon hatchling is there, it must be tethered to something or else it would quickly spread. Is it fastened to the roots of those trees that claw the air? One of the current Arkham tales is about fat oaks that shine and move as they ought not to do at night.

WHAT it is, only God knows. In terms of matter I suppose the thing Ammi described would be called a gas, but this gas obeyed laws that are not of our cosmos. This was no fruit of such worlds and suns as shine on the telescopes and photographic plates of our observatories. This was no breath from the skies whose motions and dimensions our astronomers measure or deem too vast to measure. It was just a colour out of space—a frightful messenger from unformed realms of infinity beyond all Nature as we know it; from realms whose mere existence stuns the brain and numbs us with the black extra-cosmic gulfs it throws open before our frenzied eyes.

I doubt very much if Ammi consciously lied to me, and I do not think his tale was all a freak of madness as the townfolk had forewarned. Something terrible came to the hills and valleys on that meteor, and something terrible—though I know not in what proportion—still remains. I shall be glad to see the water come. Meanwhile I hope nothing will happen to Ammi. He saw so much of the thing—and its influence was so insidious. Why has he never been able to move away? How clearly he recalled those dying words of Nahum's—"can't git away … draws ye … ye know summ'at's comin', but 'tain't no use. . . ." Ammi is such a good old man—when the reservoir gang gets to work I must write the chief engineer to keep a sharp watch on him. I would hate to think of him as the grey, twisted, brittle monstrosity which persists more and more in troubling my sleep. ∎

Retro Review
(Continued from page 138)

apartment! We got to have the same roof over our heads before we can start a thing. I'm sick to death of rooms, sharing a bath, keeping food on the window sill, using somebody else's furniture. We have to have a place of our own, an apartment that's ours, where we can live like normal humans. A room is only a cage, and the street our living room. But with a real apartment, where we can cook and live and..."

Hogwash! the washed-up boxer insists, chasing the lethal dream.

At the apex of the triangle is Detective Walt Steiner and his wife Ruth. He's skeptical of the suspicion, that Tommy Cork is being set up for a Big Sleepy Fall, but he's intrigued by the case. He, himself, was a promising young boxer who turned to police work for a steady living, and he remembers "Irish Tommy's" bouts. His wife, an author of light fiction, sees an opportunity to gather inspiration for the literary hopper.

In this respect, Tommy Cork is being used by the very people trying to help him, as well as the shifty scumbags.

My heart went out to May Cork, the Plain Jane waitress grabbing at desperate straws to solidify their rickety marriage. "Irish" Tommy Cork is a sympathetic character, chasing that dream at all costs, but he's chasing a dream limited by the frailties of human flesh — and he ain't no Rocky Balboa. There won't be an all-star fight with vindication as the prize.

The Big Fix works on many levels — hardboiled thriller, literary character study, and as a platform for Lacy/Zinberg to wax

philosophical on boxing, writing, police procedure, poverty, and love among desperate people. It also serves as a good crash-course to Ed Lacy's work. These themes are apparent in at least three other novels — *Blonde Bait*, *Breath No More My Lady*, and *The Woman Aroused*.

Once Tommy Cork stumbles away into the urban sunrise with May, I turned to *Blonde Bait* (Zenith Books, 1959). Mickey Anderson (a false name the hero gives at one point) is a sailor with his own small yacht. On an island not much good for anything except getting away from society, he meets Rose, a disheveled woman hiding from something she won't name.

They sail, fish, swim, drink, and eventually she is persuaded to go for a night on the town. Right out of a nightclub starting gate, she's recognized, and the chase is on.

Rose goes into hiding while Mickey plays amateur detective.

Breathe No More My Lady (Avon Books, 1958) presents a publishing house executive as main protagonist, investigating the death of a popular author's wife. Meanwhile, in *The Woman Aroused* (Avon, 1951), the marketing mogul at a New York publishing house investigates the murder of an Army friend — and adopts his halfwit lover, whose sexual prowess is surpassed only by her childish acts of violence.

While *Blonde Bait* depicts two vagabonds who confront the *femme's* mysterious past, after much lounging, the latter two novels feature protagonists who never really get around to protag-ing. Lacy piles on descriptions of the town, endless meals in bars or diners, visiting *amigos*.

Boxing, writing and/or sailing figure into each novel — in the main storyline, as a side character's backstory, or in as endless character conversations.

Breath No More My Lady presents a case worthy of Perry Mason, perhaps in short story form, but the final payoff is long overdue. *The Woman Aroused*, Lacy's *first* novel, is a tire that keeps going flat, no matter how much air gets pumped in.

Lacy crafts interesting characters. His observations of life, love, and career, make for vivid dressing on the hardboiled salad. Based upon this random selection, the pulp-reading aficionado may decide Lacy is hit-or-miss for plotting and pacing. ∎

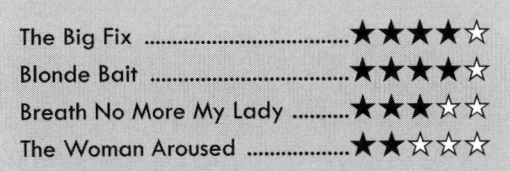

The Big Fix	★★★★☆
Blonde Bait	★★★★☆
Breath No More My Lady	★★★☆☆
The Woman Aroused	★★☆☆☆

Retro Review
by RICH HARVEY

Ed Lacy: Hit with 'Big Fix,' Miss with 'Woman Aroused'

Through the miracle of electronic editions, I sat down and read four novels by Ed Lacy, a pseudonym of Leonard S. Zinberg (1911-1968).

The Big Fix (Pyramid Books, 1960) follows three different trajectories, all leading to one point. At one corner, three scumbags plot the ringside death of a boxer, expecting to win big betting against their own sap. In the other corner is sap in question, "Irish" Tommy Cork, a middle-weight boxer who cannot accept his fate — that he's finished as a prize-fighter.

Manager Bobby Becker: "You mean you can't chance being locked out." He sighed again. "I don't know, kid, you once looked like money in the bank — a dozen years ago. If you hadn't insisted on the Robinson fight … "

Apparently, Sugar Ray Robinson handed "Irish Tommy" his head, after which Tommy never fully recovered. But the Scumbags dangle a tempting carrot of fame and riches before him, and Tommy must chase the carrot. Especially when they start doling out money.

May Cork, Tommy's estranged wife, is working a greasy spoon when they have a big confrontation. From here it's easy living, just two more years with big prize money — but May has her heart set on a

simple apartment, and a regular job for Tommy.

"… Tom, I've been thinking a lot about us. When you're lonely, you think. My sickness, the army, you away training so much, we never had our chance at happiness, really being man and wife. You know what's the key to everything? A home —an

(Continued on page 136)

Printed in Great Britain
by Amazon